MW00779892

MEND

COPYRIGHT

© 2018 Chelle Bliss
Published by Chelle Bliss

All rights reserved. No part of this book may be reproduced or transmitted in any form, including electronic or mechanical, without written permission from the publisher, except in the case of brief quotations embodied in critical articles or reviews.

This is a work of fiction. Names, characters, businesses, places, events, and incidents are either the products of the author's imagination or used in a fictitious manner. Any resemblance to actual persons, living or dead, or actual events is purely coincidental. This book is licensed for your personal enjoyment only.

This book may not be re-sold or given away to other people. If you would like to share this book with another person, please purchase an additional copy for each person you share it with. If you are reading this book and did not purchase it, or it was not purchased for your use only, then you should return it to the seller and purchase your own copy. Thank you for respecting the author's work.

Published by Chelle Bliss January 22nd 2018
Editor: Silently Correcting Your Grammar
Proofreader: Deaton Author Services
Cover Design © Chelle Bliss
Formatted by Brian Morgan
Cover Photo © Sara Eirew

—MEN OF INKED SERIES—

THROTTLE ME - Book 1

HOOK ME - Book 2

RESIST ME - Book 3

UNCOVER ME - Book 4

WITHOUT ME - Book 5

HONOR ME - Book 6

WORSHIP ME - Book 7

Men of Inked Bonus Novellas

The Gallos (Bonus Book .5)

Resisting (Bonus Book 2.5)

Men of Inked Xmas (Bonus Book 6.5)

—ALFA INVESTIGATIONS—

SINFUL INTENT - Book 1

UNLAWFUL DESIRE - Book 2

WICKED IMPULSE - Book 3

Men of Inked spin-off series!

—OTHER BLISS BOOKS—

MISADVENTURES OF A CITY GIRL

ENSHRINE

REBOUND

TOP BOTTOM SWITCH

DIRTY WORK

DIRTY SECRET

—TAKEOVER DUET—

ACQUISITION - TAKEOVER DUET 1

MERGER - TAKEOVER DUET 2

—LOVE AT LAST SERIES—

UNTANGLE ME - Book 1

KAYDEN THE PAST - Book 2

To learn more about Chelle's books visit *chellebliss.com*

FOREWORD

As I sit here on January 5, 2018 and type this foreword almost a year has passed since I finished the first draft of Mend.

I watched him slowly grow weaker, but tried to continued to keep writing. The once strong man that was my first super hero could barely walk anymore and it broke me. The cancer that filled his body was winning and no matter how hard he fought, it was a losing battle.

I remember almost every moment of January 28, 2017, the day I typed *The End* in this book and I don't ever want to forget it either.

I sat by my father's beside with my knees up around my chest and tried not to break down into tears while he laid on his side, staring at me with a sweet smile like he often did. "Did you finish your book?"

I scooted forward and rested my chin on the mattress. "I did, Daddy."

"Good," he said and winced as he adjusted his legs.

"Can I do something?" I asked, feeling completely helpless and heartbroken.

"No. I'm okay."

That was my dad. He never complained about anything. He was the most caring and supportive man I've ever known. I was truly blessed to have him in my life and wish I could've held on to him a little longer, but some things aren't meant to be.

"Are you sure?"

He touched my nose and smiled again, trying to pretend he wasn't in pain. "Go home and start the next book."

"I can't do that, Daddy," I said as tears threatened to fall.

"It's important that you start the next one."

I somehow muttered the words, "It's not important."

"It is important."

"It's not more important than you."

"It is."

"It's not," I told him and I wasn't about to cave.

There isn't anything more important than my family, especially my father. I would've given up everything I had, including my career, if it meant I could have him in my life for a little while longer.

Eight months earlier we buried my brother and my father watched me struggle with my words along with my life every day since. I'm sure he knew I'd be unable to write much of anything without him in my life.

My father closed his eyes, facing in my direction as I

leaned against the wall and watched him sleep. I sat in silence, crying without a sound because I didn't want to wake him.

That was the day I knew my father would die. I wasn't ready, but then again, can we ever be prepared?

For the next three nights, I laid at his side and held his hand, running my fingers through his hair as he struggled to breathe and fought to stay with us just a little while longer. He didn't sleep and neither did I. I couldn't waste each precious minute I had left with my father on something as frivolous as sleep. I played him his favorite songs, talked to him non-stop, and cried when he couldn't see me anymore.

When he took his last breath, my world changed forever. The heartache of losing a parent is indescribable, unescapable, and all consuming. Even today, a year later, I'm a shell of my former self and I'm not sure I'll ever find the happiness I had before…when my father was in my life.

Mend, the book you're about to read, was the book I finished right before my father passed. It's the last one he ever knew I was writing. I couldn't open the book for months. Every time I did and tried to read through it, I had to close the document because there was too much emotion and memories tied to the words.

In all honesty, Mend was a hot mess. I knew my dad was dying while I wrote the book. I couldn't think clearly. Every day before I started to write, I'd have to go back and re-read my previous words. I no longer had the ability to remember anything I'd written the day before. Instead of pushing Mend out, I put it aside and didn't think about opening it again until December 2017.

The document sat on my desktop, taunting me in a way. I couldn't leave it there any longer to linger in obscurity. With the help of my friend, Glenna Maynard, I decided that I could finally dive back into Mend and complete the book I'd promised my daddy I finished.

Mend may not be the panty scorcher I'd intended it to be. When I started writing Mend, I planned on this to be Maneuver which has a smoking hot cover. But ultimately, that's not what I wrote. To be fair to readers, I changed the name and found a more appropriate cover. No longer am I willing to keep the book to myself and am finally ready to share my words with you.

The story is no less beautiful even though it's not filled with sexy scenes. It's a story of lost love, misunderstandings, and second chances. Sometimes I don't have control of the words that pour out of me and Mend is a perfect example of that. I never intended to write this book, but my brain had other plans. The characters often rule me more than I have power over them.

I hope you enjoy the story of Jack and Evie as much as I do. Thank you for sticking by my side the last year and being patient with me as I try to find my words again.

I keep writing not because I can, I write to honor the memory of my father and to make him prouder than he was when he breathed his last breath.

I write for you, too. Without readers such as yourself, I may have totally lost my way.

I'm slowly finding my groove again and I just know 2018 will be an amazing year of books and tons of words.

I apologize for any typos. I wanted to share my feelings and added this just before publishing. Sorry, Lisa.

Love Always,

Chelle Bliss, xoxo

To the only sister I've ever known…
I love you, Kelly. - Chelle

PROLOGUE

I gaze up at her from where I'm kneeling on the floor with my fists clenched so tightly my fingertips ache. My vision blurs as her words sink in. "You can't go."

Sitting on the edge of my bed, she holds her tiny face in her hands as tears fall between her fingers, landing on my jeans. "My dad got his orders weeks ago but never told me until tonight. We leave tomorrow, Jack." Her voice cracks on my name.

I swallow, desperately trying to process the information yet not wanting to believe it at the same time. "Tomorrow?" Panic starts to settle in my bones. "You can't leave now."

"I have to." She lifts her eyes to mine in a silent plea and apology.

I wipe the tears from her cheeks, wishing we could run away and leave our lives behind. "Maybe you can stay with me." I refuse to let her walk out of my life. We're so close to being free of her father, only nine months from graduation.

Shaking her head, she whispers, "I can't." Her bottom lip trembles as she squeezes her eyes shut. "I don't know what I'm going to do without you."

"I'll talk to my mom. She knows we love each other, Evie." My throat starts to close, and I feel like I'm suffocating at the thought of her not being here. Evie opens her mouth to say something, but I stop her. "Don't give up." I hold her hands in mine, caressing the soft skin with my thumb, and search her eyes for a glimmer of hope.

"My dad will never go for it. You know that."

I grip her hands tighter and shake my head. I'm unable to believe we only have tonight. "There has to be something we can do."

"I have to go, but it's only for a year," she whispers softly, barely able to look me in the eyes. "I'll come back."

"I can't wait a year. I'll visit you every weekend."

"Jack," she says as more tears fall, turning her head away from me. "We're moving to Germany."

Her words punch me in the gut, almost knocking me backward. "Germany?" I stammer.

Her father's moving her to another continent, halfway across the world, and it's entirely because of me. He's hated me from the moment he found out Evie and I were dating.

"In a year, we'll graduate, and we can be together forever." I refuse to believe this will be the end for us. Evie and I have plans...a future.

"I'll come back to you," she promises, resting her hand on top of mine as I grip her cheeks and gaze into her blue eyes.

She's everything to me.

I try to memorize every detail of her face. The blueness of her eyes and how they match the sky just as the sun meets the horizon on a summer evening. The flecks of brown in her blond hair that turn auburn in the sunlight and how those silky strands feel wrapped around my fingers. Near the corner of her right eye, she has the tiniest collection of freckles resembling the Big Dipper. There's no one more beautiful than her.

She's become part of me.

My other half.

The first thought I have every morning and the last every single night before I close my eyes is of Evie. My chest tightens at the thought of not seeing her every day.

When she leaves, what will be left?

How can there be an us if we aren't even in the same country?

Evie being my girl is all I've ever known. She's as much a part of me as the air I breathe.

I love this girl more than life itself.

"How long do we have?"

She nestles her face into my hand and closes her eyes. "He gave me an hour to say goodbye. If it weren't for my mom, I wouldn't even be getting this. You know how he can be."

"It's not goodbye, Evie. I can never say goodbye to you. We'll see each other again. I promise you."

"I'll love you always, Jack. I promise I'll come back to you. I'll be back before you have time to miss me."

I miss her already, and she's right in front of me. I don't know how I am going to do this. How do I let her go? I'm terrified that once she walks out this door, it is going to be the last time I see her.

"I'll wait an eternity for you, Evie. I'll never stop loving you. Just come back to me, no matter how long it takes. I'll be here waiting."

"I promise." She flings herself into my arms, needing my touch as desperately as I crave hers.

We're holding each other so tightly that I can barely breathe, but it doesn't matter. All I want is for Evie to stay.

She's mine.

I never want to let her go.

Not like this.

Not before our last year in school.

We made plans.

Shared our dreams.

I breathe in the scent of her strawberry shampoo, committing the smell to memory. Not that I could ever forget anything about my Evie girl. She's unforgettable.

"I don't want to cry anymore," she whispers in my ear and grabs the back of my hair, tangling it between her fingers. Those soft lips I have tasted so many times brush over mine, full of desperation, matching my own.

We fall back onto my bed as I kick off my shoes and pull my shirt over my head. I need to feel her skin-to-skin. I try to push away the thought that this could be the last time I hold her in my arms. This could be the last time I taste her lips. This could be the last time she is truly mine.

"God, I love you, Evie."

"I love you too," she whispers as I cover her body with mine.

JACK

SIX YEARS LATER

Asphyxiation.

It's the only word that describes how I feel in this very moment. Setting eyes on Evie—my first girlfriend—the only girl I've ever loved, feels like strong hands wrapping around my throat, squeezing with such intensity that I'm suffocating.

"Hey." My little sister, Myra, appears in my peripheral vision. She nudges me in the side with her sharp elbow when I don't respond. "You okay?"

"No."

The way Evie's hair is blowing in the wind, licking her shoulders with each sweep of the unseasonably warm spring air has my dick stirring like she stepped straight out of a wet dream. She's laughing and holding her stomach as she talks to some guy—a man I've never seen before.

I want to run over there, throw her over my shoulder, and claim her in front of the entire town, but I'm in shock and can't bring myself to move.

I can't help but stare at her long legs and remember the way they felt wrapped around me the last time we were together. When I made love to her for the *last* time. The promises we made reverberate in the back of my mind. *"I promise, Jack..."* Her voice is still so clear inside my head.

Myra takes a step forward, and her cotton candy tumbles to the dirt in front of her. "Son of a fuck," she whispers, finally seeing Evie.

"Watch your mouth," I growl.

"Is that…" Her voice trails off because it's like we've both seen a ghost.

Swallowing the lump that's lodged in my throat doesn't make my ability to breathe any easier. "Yeah."

"Well, Jesus." Myra moves in front of me and tries to get my attention with a shove to my chest. When I don't budge, she grabs my face and forces my eyes to her. "What do you want to do? I'll go kick her ass if you want."

"Myra." I remove her hands from my face as my gaze drifts away from Evie. "Do *not* make a scene."

Myra Nelson is a whopping five feet two, but she has the attitude of an NFL linebacker. Even as a little girl, she walked around the house crashing into everything on purpose just to watch it crumble in her wake, and she hasn't stopped sixteen years later.

She crosses her arms in front of her chest and scowls. "I never make a scene. But I would for you," she sasses, pitching a thumb over her shoulder in Evie's direction. "Especially when it comes to *her*."

"What happened is between Evie and me." I know I need to de-escalate the situation before Myra goes apeshit. "Ma would have a fit if you got in trouble."

She rolls her eyes. "I don't give a crap. Some things need to happen, no matter the consequence."

I focus my gaze on Myra's, tightening my grip on her shoulders. "You will not do or say a thing, or I'll carry you straight home."

Her mahogany eyes sparkle in the sunlight as she takes a step forward, getting in my face. "You wouldn't dare," she hisses with all the attitude of a teenage girl.

Leaning forward, I drop my voice to a whisper so low only she can hear me. "In a fuckin' heartbeat. Go find your friends, and forget you saw her."

I can tell she wants to say something, and it's hanging on the tip of her tongue. "Fine. But…"

"But nothing. Just go. Do as you're told for once." I tip my chin to the midway behind her. "Ride something."

A smile spreads across her face, and she quirks an eyebrow. "Anything?"

I instantly regret the carelessness in my word choice. "A damn ride, Myra. Go be a kid instead of a pain in my ass."

"I'm sixteen, Jack." She pokes me in the chest with her bony finger. "You can't control me anymore." Her glittery painted fingernail starts to bite into my skin, and I growl.

As if I ever could. But I tried like hell to keep her out of trouble. Once Myra began to develop breasts, every boy in town wanted a piece of her. I made sure everyone knew I'd break their fingers if they touched her, and so far, I haven't had an issue.

"How much will it take for you to go away?"

I'm done with her bullshit, and there's only one thing that gets her ass moving—money.

She rubs her chin like she's deep in thought, but we both know how much she's going to ask me to give her. "Hmm. A hundred bucks." The corner of her mouth turns up into a smile because she thinks she's won, but I would've paid her twice as much to get rid of her.

Reaching into my pocket, I pull out a wad of cash, plucking a bill off the stack and fanning it in front of her face. "Don't find me for an hour. Do not go near Evie either. Disappear, Myra. Got it?"

She salutes me before snatching the hundred from my fingers and stuffing it in her bra. "One hour. Anything more will cost you." Spinning around on her heels, she stalks off toward the cotton candy stand, kicking the dirt-covered sugar puff across the midway as she walks.

I turn my attention back to Evie. The guy has his arms wrapped around her waist, whispering something in her ear. Her hands rest on his shoulders as she laughs. My fists tighten at my sides at their public display.

I loved her from the moment she walked into home-room on the first day of eighth grade. The fact that she had on a Nirvana T-shirt and a pair of ripped jeans just made me fall even harder.

Now she stands only feet in front me, a little taller and a little more well-endowed, but still…she causes my heart to beat out of control.

When the guy spins Evie around, I get my first full glimpse of her face in six years, and the small amount of air in my lungs evaporates. Every muscle in my body tenses, and I'm momentarily frozen as I take her in. My need to talk to her overtakes all rational thought, and I head straight toward her as if I'm on autopilot.

As she makes another rotation in his arms, Evie's eyes lock on mine. Her mesmerizing blue eyes go wide as she turns her head, following me as I stalk toward her.

Picking up my pace with each step, I move through the crowd with ease.

She wiggles free of his embrace as I get closer, pushing against the guy's shoulders. For a moment, I think she's going to run to me and jump in my arms because she has missed me as much as I have missed her, but when her feet touch the ground…

She takes off in the opposite direction.

As I chase after her, the crowd surges inward, closing the gap as if they're trying to keep us apart.

"Evie, wait!" I reach for her even though she's too far away. The thought of touching her after all this time sends a shiver down my spine.

Peering over her shoulder, she glances back with tear-stained cheeks, no longer smiling. Her body's moving forward, propelling her farther away, but her eyes never leave mine.

"Evie!" I plead for her to stop, but she doesn't.

I know what's about to happen, and there's nothing I can do to stop it. She's moving too fast for me to even scream a warning. Her body bounces backward as she hits the parade float and collapses on the grass.

People rush to her side, but I don't want anyone to touch her…only me. I push them away, layer after layer of nervous and nosy bystanders, until her motionless body is at my feet.

She's knocked out cold.

"Everyone back up." I urge them to make way,

sweeping my arms in a circle over her body. Stealing a glance at her, I kneel at her side. Even out cold and with blood running from the gash in her head, she is the most beautiful woman I've ever laid eyes on. "Evie," I whisper hoarsely, desperate for her to look at me.

My heart's in my throat, pounding so fast that I wonder if the people around me can hear it as clearly as I can.

I stroke her damp cheek with the backs of my knuckles. "Evie, wake up. Please, wake up for me, sweetheart."

EVIE

I'm comfortable in the darkness—it's warm and consuming in its nothingness—and every fucked-up thing in my life has melted away.

"Evie." His voice cuts like a knife, reopening every wound I've tried so hard to heal. Nothing could have prepared me to see *him* again.

I'm not ready to open my eyes and face Jack, not yet. I want to stay here in the void where I don't have to confront the man who broke my heart.

Jack promised he'd wait for me, that he'd always love me, but he lied. Instead, he broke every promise he made me.

My head throbs, and everything is spinning like I've had too much to drink. The voices around me grow louder before fading away again.

"Evie, wake up," Jack pleads. When he touches my cheek, the tiny hairs on the back of my neck stand, and my skin pebbles with goose bumps, just like it did when we were together.

"Should we call an ambulance?" a woman asks in the distance.

"No," he growls all possessively, claiming his ownership like he did when we were kids.

Jack doesn't own me. Not anymore.

Man, I fucked up good.

The moment we locked eyes, I knew I had to run. After what happened, I couldn't face him. My mistake wasn't running away from him; it was my inability to resist catching one last glimpse of his beautiful face—the same one that has haunted my dreams for the last six years.

I know I can't lie here forever, and Jack isn't going to walk away until I do. There's no way around it. I have to face him.

My eyes flutter open, slowly blinking to adjust to the sunlight as I stare up at him. "Jack," I whisper, unable to resist saying his name. A name that has brought me so much pleasure and pain. A name I have tried so hard and failed to forget.

"Evie." He smiles, exhaling a sigh of relief. When I try to sit up, he gently pushes me back down. "Don't move." His face is soft as his eyes search mine. "Are you okay?"

I turn my head, averting my gaze because it hurts too much to look at him. "I'm fine."

That's not true. I'm crumbling into a thousand pieces on the inside. I remember the way he looked at me as though I was the only girl in the world who mattered to him. That wasn't true, though. It was all lies. The promises we made meant nothing to him. His actions proved that long ago, and yet, being here with him now, all those feelings and memories bubble to the surface.

"I love you, Evie. This isn't goodbye…"

I thought he'd love me forever, but it didn't take him very long to move on after I left. When he did, he ripped my heart out, leaving a gaping hole in its place. Jack shattered me and every illusion I had about love. He destroyed me in the worst possible way.

He deserted me.

His hand slides down my side, resting just above the waistband of my shorts. His touch is intimate and shouldn't cause a thrill of pleasure to shoot through me, but it does and that terrifies me. "Are you sure? Wiggle your toes."

"I'm fine, Jack."

His grip tightens, but I ignore the silent warning. My hand pushes against his chest but lingers a little too long.

Good Lord.

He's huge.

Even after all these years, he still takes my breath away. I shouldn't fawn over him. I know it, but I can't stop myself. Six years is a long time without laying eyes on the man I loved—and if I'm being honest, I still haven't gotten over.

Everything about his face is the same. I memorized every inch of it down to the dip in the middle of his top lip that creates the perfect M. Somehow, his nose is still straight and perfectly symmetrical even after all the times I saw his face take a punch. His chiseled jawline and high cheekbones are more pronounced than I remember, but it's his eyes with their piercing blue color that captivate me.

He leans back, ripping the shirt from his body. He mirrors something straight out of an all-male revue. I gawk at him openmouthed, unable to find my words as if I've never seen a bare chest before.

Jesus.

I blink a few times, but I can't stop staring at him. He's perfect in every way but one—he lied to me. Every time he moves, his muscles ripple and the sunlight bounces off his golden-tanned skin, turning me into a bumbling idiot.

I push myself off the ground and start to sway. I don't know if I'm dizzy from the hit or lust. Maybe both.

Grabbing my arm, he steadies me and presses his torn T-shirt against my head. He's like a superhero, swooping in to save me like a damsel in distress. Only I'm not his to save anymore. "Keep this against your wound, and I'll carry you."

I gawk at him.

It's all I can do.

Jack is really here and trying to take care of me like he cares about me at all.

The fact that I'm standing next to him is still surreal. If it weren't for the fact that he's touching me, I wouldn't believe my own eyes. I've craved his touch for so long, despite the pain it brings me.

He lifts me into his arms, and the air surges out of my lungs when our bodies collide. He's holding me against his chest—the same rock-hard chest I spent way too long staring at.

"Relax," he tells me.

Like that's going to happen.

My senses are in overdrive with the side of my body plastered against his; my skin tingles at the contact.

I'm so screwed.

How Jack still affects me like this, I'll never understand. I've spent so long convincing myself that I hated him, when it was all a big lie. One minute in his arms and I can't escape the fact that I still love him. I've always loved him. I'm on the verge of hyperventilating as my head spins out of control.

He holds me tighter, pushing my head under his chin as he carries me down the midway toward the parking lot. "I'll take care of you," he promises.

A promise I've heard before.

I'm woozy, but being in his arms is like being home again. A calmness comes over me as I snuggle into his embrace. His gentle demeanor and strong hold make me forget about everything that's happened. I could melt into his granite-hard chest and stay this way forever. Warm and protected in his arms.

What's wrong with me?

I'm not with the man five minutes, and I'm already forgetting his broken promises.

He never even said he was sorry.

He just stopped writing and never thought about me again before banging most of the girls at Ridge Hollow High.

Renee, my best friend, made sure to fill me in on every gory detail even when I didn't want to hear it. Eventually, I stopped talking to her too because I couldn't take the constant reminder of what I'd lost any longer.

He leans forward, and every dip and ridge of his

abdomen scrape against my side as he sets me on the tailgate of a pickup truck. I bite down on my lip to stop the tiny wanton moan that wants to break free.

"Let me look at your head." He gently turns my face to the side with his fingers.

In the distance, the Ferris wheel is turning, and the riders are screaming with excitement. Kind of like my insides at the close proximity of Jack.

Traitor.

"Evie!" Evan jogs toward us, his eyes moving between Jack and me.

Oh God. Evan.

Jack has me so distracted that I forgot about Evan. I'm officially the world's shittiest friend.

"Who's he?" Jack asks, and based on his tone, he isn't happy.

"Evan." I keep it short and super vague.

It isn't any of Jack's business anyway. He gave up any right to be privy to the intimate details of my life when he let me go.

I'm guessing he thinks Evan and I are a couple because he's growling like a bear about to attack. I have to suppress a small smile threatening to appear at the thought of Jack being jealous. It serves him right. He deserves it after the way he treated me.

"Who the hell are you?" Evan asks Jack like I'm not even sitting here.

"Jack," he grunts without taking his eyes off me. The intensity directed at me is overwhelming.

I widen my eyes, silently pleading with Evan to help

me out of this situation. He knows all about Jack. About our past. About my heartbreak.

Evan's eyes narrow as he pushes Jack's shoulder. "I've got her."

He doesn't budge and snarls at Evan. "I've got her."

Evan isn't backing down and tries to nudge Jack out of the way again, but Jack doesn't move. Evan's effort accomplishes nothing.

Uh oh.

This could go from bad to clusterfuck in about three seconds.

Don't get me wrong. Evan's built like a brick shithouse too, and they'd probably go a few rounds before someone would have to give in or get knocked out.

If Evan weren't gay, I totally would've swooned over him when we met. In fact, I think I did until he made it quite clear I didn't have the bits and pieces he was interested in. It doesn't hurt that he's drop-dead gorgeous and covered in muscle—not Jack-size muscle, but hard just the same.

Jack's fingertips continue moving through my hair, delicately checking the spot I assume is bleeding like a faucet because I can feel the wetness in my hair.

Placing his fingers under my chin, Jack forces me to meet his gaze. "You're going to need a stitch or two," he tells me like Evan isn't even here. "I can take you to see Dr. Carlyle."

I give Evan a sideways glance, hoping for a little backup. "Evan will take me."

Jack turns to face Evan, sizing him up with flared nostrils, daring Evan to challenge him.

Evan widens his stance, folding his arms in front of his chest to put on a show of virility. “She isn’t yours anymore, Jack. She’s none of your concern. I’ll take her.”

I give Evan a halfhearted smile because he’s trying to rescue me, but I know Jack well enough to know he’s not going to back down so easily.

“Evie will always be my concern,” Jack says, stepping toward Evan.

Oh boy.

“You lost that right a long time ago.” Evan moves forward, and they’re less than a foot apart.

“Like hell, I did!” Jack’s voice is raised.

This is going south fast. I rush to my feet, scrambling to make myself a human shield between them even though I’m half their size and dizzy as hell.

“Boys.” I press my palms against their chests, trying to keep them apart. “Let’s calm down.” I smile nervously, my eyes moving between them. “Jack.” I see the fire in his eyes, alerting me to defuse the situation before someone gets hurt. “Thank you for helping me.”

His face softens as he glances down at me. “You’re welcome, Evie.”

My heart aches at his beauty, but I remind myself he’s not mine anymore.

He hurt me.

“But.” My fingers press into Jack’s chest, relishing the feel of his smooth but hard muscles underneath my skin. “While I appreciate your offer, I’m here with Evan, and I’m not your responsibility.”

Evan’s arm coils around my back, pulling me away from Jack. He rests his hand on my hip, claiming me as if I were his own. "I got her, man. Why don't you help someone who wants it?"

I elbow him in the ribs. "Stop," I whisper, but it's too late.

"Say that again," Jack grits through his teeth, moving forward.

I give Jack's chest a hard shove. "Just go. Please."

"This is what you want?" Jack gawks at me like I've got two heads.

He's wounded by my words. I can see it. I know his expressions better than anyone's in the world, but I can't believe he's surprised after what happened between us.

I back up with Evan, trying to sell the lie. "It is." I freeze when I feel Evan's cock pressing into my ass, knowing his display of sexual prowess is not for me either.

Evan's attracted to Jack. I figured as much. I mean, who wouldn't think Jack's the complete package—minus the broody asshole part.

I wish things were different. I wish he would've waited for me. I meant every word I said to him when I left Ridge Hollow, and I haven't loved anyone since.

Jack narrows his gaze, and for a second, I think he can read my mind. "Fine," he says, finally backing down.

"Take this," I say, holding out his blood-soaked T-shirt for him to take.

"Keep it." Jack swipes his tongue across his bottom lip, and my eyes follow, wondering if they still taste and feel the same. "Bye, Evie girl," he says with a slight smirk, and I know I've been caught staring when he uses the name he called me a million times before.

Oh, no.

"Bye," I whisper before turning around because I can't look at him another minute without wanting to run into his arms and kiss those lips that I've dreamed about for far too long.

"Don't look back," Evan whispers once we're away from Jack's truck.

"I won't."

He leans over with his arm flung around my shoulders, putting on a full display of heterosexual nonsense while we're walking across the parking lot. "He's hot though, Evie."

"Yep. I know." I laugh even though the motion makes me wince at the dull pain stemming from my head because Evan's whiskers are tickling my ear. "I felt how much you liked him," I tease, attempting to ignore the pain.

"Hell, I had to hide behind you because I couldn't conceal it anymore."

"Figured that's why you were standing behind me, especially when I felt *that* thing stabbing me in the back. He's totally your type."

Evan pulls me closer, putting his arm around my shoulder. "He's our type." He laughs before kissing the top of my head, forgetting about my gash. "Shit, sorry." He backs away and flinches when he catches a glimpse of the wound. "That's a deep cut. Where do we go?"

"Not Carlyle. Take me to the urgent care in Hunter."

"Why not Carlyle?"

"'Cause Jack will be looking for me."

"Would he really?"

"Yep." I climb on Evan's scooter and pat the seat in

front of me with a glare. "Don't get any ideas either, buddy."

"I would never do that to you." He smirks over his shoulder as he slides onto the seat in front of me. "But can I have his shirt when you're done?"

"Um, no." I jam the black T-shirt, half soaked in blood and the other half covered in his scent, into the back pocket of my shorts. "Just drive before he comes after us," I bark, eager to be away from here.

Away from the temptation Jack presents. Being near him is dangerous for my heart.

"I don't know if the scooter is the best idea after you took a hit like that."

"I'm fine, Evan. Just drive, and get me the hell out of here." I close my eyes and wrap my arms around him to stop myself from sneaking a last glance at Jack.

For a moment…I let myself pretend it's Jack I'm holding on to as we pull away.

JACK

Myra kicks at the dirt near my truck. She's hunched over with a pout that could almost pull at my heartstrings if I didn't know what a con artist she can be. "Do you have to leave now? Shit was just starting to get good."

Ridge Hollow's buzzing with the news that Evie and I finally crossed paths after six years apart. In a town this small, that's considered a big deal. There's even videos of it swirling around social media with the hashtag #TogetherAgain. Myra was more than happy to shove them in my face on her cell phone.

"I have to check on the business and tie up some loose ends, but I promise I won't be long."

She peers up at me with her big brown eyes that make her look shockingly sweet and innocent. "You comin' back for Evie?"

"You want me to come back for Evie?"

Myra crosses her arms and sighs. "If it means you'd be back in the Hollow, then yes."

"Aww, you missin' me?"

"Not so much," she teases. "You've taken some of the heat off me since you've been here, though." A grin spreads across her face.

She's such a brat.

"Nice, Myra."

She steps back, patting my truck door as I start the engine. "Better hurry. Evie may not be here forever."

Her words and their severity don't sink in until after I've pulled onto the highway.

For six hours, I think about nothing except Evie. Seeing her again has changed everything.

With endless miles of nothing but corn rows and the open road, I think about the couple we used to be.

My palms are sweating, worrying that she'll pull away when I ask her. Wiping the dampness on the front of my jeans as I try to control my breathing. I don't want to ruin the friendship we've formed, but I know what I want...and it's only her.

Evie and I have been hanging out after school almost every day—at least, when her dad lets her. He's a real hard-ass.

Since she's attended Hollow Middle, at least half a dozen guys have asked her to be their girlfriend. To my surprise, she's turned every single one down, but I'm not letting that deter me, though.

I'm different from the other guys, and I've taken the time to get to know her before trying to claim her as mine.

"Evie!" I yell when I see her come running down the steps after school.

God, she's beautiful.

Her ponytail is swaying from side to side as she bounces down the steps, heading right toward me with a giant smile spreading across her face when she spots me.

"Down here." I wave my arms frantically, and she waves back.

Holding the railing, she turns to her friend Renee, giggling as they glance down at me. Evie's wearing cutoff jean shorts, a vintage rock band T-shirt, and Converse sneakers.

"Hey," I say, tucking my hands into my front pockets.

"Hey, Jack," Renee says with a smirk.

I hate her, but I can't be a complete asshole because she's Evie's friend.

I give her a short nod because Evie's watching me. "Renee."

"What are you two doing today?" Renee asks, twirling her fingers in her hair and chomping on her gum like a cow.

"I thought we'd head out into the woods behind my house."

"Ick," she mutters and makes a sour face, always being the judgmental bitch. "Who wants to traipse around in the forest? It's so last year." She rolls her eyes at the absurdity of my idea.

Renee is such a snob, and I don't understand why Evie hangs around with her.

"I love hiking," Evie admits even though it earns her a dirty look from her BFF, Renee Callahan.

"Well, I'm going to go shopping and meet Jess for ice cream."

Jess is Renee's boyfriend, and they're both totally annoying and complete assholes. They're perfect for each other.

"Have fun with the leaves and shit." Renee reaches into her purse and pulls out her roll-on lip gloss. She sweeps it across her lips three times before smacking them together. "Toodles," she says, waving over her shoulder as she heads down the path where Jess is waiting for her with his friends.

I gaze at Evie as she watches Renee walk away, and for a moment, I can't speak. I'm so nervous, and she's so beautiful. I wonder if I'll end up ruining everything. "Did you want to go for ice cream instead?"

"No." She shakes her head, bringing her eyes back to mine. "I want to be outside." She smiles at me.

I'm glad that she's nothing like Renee. Even if Renee had Evie's beauty, I could never tolerate her elitist attitude and cattiness. Being around that girl even five minutes is mentally exhausting.

"Good. We can drop our things on my porch before we go," I tell her, and my heart picks up, knowing that soon I'll ask her an important question. One I've been waiting to ask for a month. I swallow hard at the realization that in just under an hour, I'll ask Evie to be my girlfriend, and she might actually say yes.

"Anything you want." She smiles again, and her cheeks turn a rosy shade of pink.

I like the sound of that, but I like everything she says.

We walk outside, an eerie silence hanging between us

as we wander toward the sidewalk that leads to my house. "What time do your parents want you home?" I ask, breaking up the quiet and wishing I had balls enough to ask her now.

"Dinner's at seven. I can't be late, or I'll be grounded for a week."

"That's fine."

I'm disappointed because it's already three. I hate school days. They suck the life out of everything fun. I want to spend every free moment with Evie.

When we're far enough away from the school and completely alone, I reach down and tuck her hand in mine. She doesn't pull away or look at me, but I can see her tiny smile even though her face is shrouded by her hair.

"Is this okay?" I squeeze her hand, seeking the affirmation that I haven't overstepped some imaginary line.

"It's good." She bites her lip and glances over her shoulder at me. "I like it."

I breathe a little easier, but holding her hand is only the first step in my plan to make Evie my girl. Before I left for school this morning, I packed us a picnic and gave my mom strict instructions not to touch anything.

Mom laughed and said I'd watched too many romantic movies with her. She also said I was too young to have a girlfriend, followed by her saying, "You should enjoy your youth."

Whatever that means. We're thirteen. Old enough to know what we want and who we are. Youth isn't all that great anyway. We spend our days in school being bossed around, only to come home and be bossed around again but in a completely different way. I can't wait to be older to gain some freedom and not have to listen to another person tell me to sit down, shut up, do your chores, and everything else adults order kids to do.

None of it matters. The thing that makes me the happiest is Evie, and she's at my side after I run into the house, grabbing the picnic basket without even so much as a word to my mother. Myra will be home in a few minutes, and the last thing I need is her tagging along.

"Do you like it?" I ask as the path ends and the woods open into a sprawling field with a vast lake in the center.

The trees around the water have started to turn the most beautiful shades of red, orange, and yellow. The wildflowers that surround the shore have begun to die off, but the scenery resembles a majestic postcard. The sun's rays reflect off the lake, almost blinding us, and mirrored on the water's surface is an exact duplicate of the sight before us.

Her eyes sweep over the landscape, but my eyes are only on her. "It's beautiful," she whispers with her hand above her eyes, shielding them from the sun. "I don't know if I've ever seen anything more beautiful."

"I have."

Nothing in the world is more beautiful than her.

She turns to me, her forehead lined with tiny wrinkles, confused by my words. "What?"

"It's stunning," I say, but I'm talking about her face even though I motion toward the lake with my hand.

She takes a few steps toward the lake, pulling me by my hand, and stops at the water's edge. "Why didn't you show me this earlier?"

I shrug and regret that I didn't. "I didn't know you were into this type of thing."

"Jack, I'm not like the other girls."

"I know." My heart's racing, pounding loudly in my chest, and I wonder if she can hear it like I can. "Evie?" My stomach starts to flip. I have to ask her now before I chicken out. This is the perfect moment.

"Yeah?" She tucks a few strands of her golden hair that have been blown by the wind behind her ear.

Taking a deep breath, I simply throw it out there. "Will you be my girlfriend?" My words come out fast. When she doesn't answer right away, I turn my body to face her. Our hands are still connected, and my palms begin to sweat again. "I want you to be my girl."

Turning toward me with a crooked smile, she blinks slowly. "I want to be yours, Jack. I've never wanted anything more."

I exhale, relief flooding through my system, and adrenaline taking over. "Hell yeah!" I fist-pump the air.

"I've been waiting for you to ask," she admits softly.

My mouth falls open at my stupidity for waiting so long. "You have?"

"You're my best friend. There's no one else I want."

"I am?"

I thought Renee was her bestie, but clearly, I was wrong.

"Renee is just so…" She shakes her head. "She only knows one side of me, but you know all of me."

I'm smiling so big my cheeks hurt, and the passion of her statement cascades over me like a warm shower. Dropping the picnic basket next to my feet, I reach up and put my hands against her cheeks. "All the guys are going to be jealous of me at school tomorrow."

She giggles, pushing her face into one of my palms. "The girls that don't hate me already will for sure when they find out."

"They will?" I brush my thumbs up and down her cheeks.

"You're quite the catch."

"Sure…" I take a step closer, and my heart beats faster, my breathing ragged. "Can I kiss you?"

I've never kissed anyone except for my mom and sister, but I want nothing more than to plant my lips against Evie's and taste that strawberry lip gloss she's always spreading across them.

"I've never kissed anyone before." She frowns, biting down gently on her bottom lip.

"Me either. Don't worry. We'll figure it out," I tell her as I lean in and press my mouth to hers.

EVIE

"Ms. Bailey," the nurse calls out.

I've been flipping through an old copy of *Ladies' Home Journal* magazine, with Jack's T-shirt pressed against my head, for the last hour as Evan clicked away on his phone. My ass is numb from sitting in the waiting room for so long. My legs hurt, my head aches, and I'm a complete mess by the time it's my turn to go back.

I don't even remember the pages I've just browsed through. The whole time I sat here, all I could think about was Jack.

The way it felt when we touched. The way his voice traveled over my body, caressing every nerve. I've been on edge, drowning in the memories of who we used to be. I can't help but wonder what kind of man he has become.

Evan grabs my hand to steady me when my legs almost give out. "Want me to come?" he asks.

"Yes. Please."

I begged him to put a Band-Aid on it to see if it would stop bleeding on its own, but Evan refused. I've never liked needles and have gone out of my way to avoid them, but Evan isn't having any of it.

He holds my hand as we follow the nurse down the beige hallway. I try not to fidget when every part of my body wants to run in the opposite direction.

"Wait in here," she says, pushing open the last door on the right. "The doctor will be with you shortly." Her gaze lingers on Evan for a moment before she leaves us alone.

"So…" Evan peers up at me from the chair against the wall as I climb onto the exam table. "Jack."

I start to hum, ignoring the topic he's been dying to ask me about since we arrived. The waiting room was too busy for him to pry, but now that we're alone, he's going to pester me. I kick my feet against the bottom of the table and keep humming, staring down at the floor.

"Evie," he presses.

I sigh loudly and finally look in his direction. "I don't want to talk about him."

"We're going to talk about him. You said he was handsome, but you never told me he was the hottest man on Earth."

"He's not all that, Ev," I say, somehow keeping a straight face.

Evan rolls his eyes. "Please tell me he has a micropeen."

"I needed a microscope to find it." I nod, but heat creeps into my cheeks as I remember the beauty that is Jack Nelson's dick. Even after six years, I haven't forgotten one delectable inch.

“You’re an asshole.”

We laugh until there’s a knock on the door, and I straighten, fear seeping into my bones.

“Ms. Bailey,” the doctor greets me, stepping into the room as he stares down at a clipboard.

“That’s me.” My gaze slides to Evan, and I give him an awkward fake smile. I’m so nervous, and my feet are moving so fast that I’m practically running in midair.

Evan’s busy checking out the doctor, appraising his features like he does with every man we come across. He’s become thoroughly impressed with the “stock,” as he calls it, of Ridge Hollow.

He has a thing for country boys.

The doctor glances up and gives me a small smile before looking down at the paperwork again. “I see you’re here because you hit your head.”

“Yep.” I gnaw on the inside of my cheek and start to rock back and forth.

The doctor isn’t much older than I am, and I can’t imagine he’s been out of medical school for very long. I was hoping for someone more mature with a little more experience under his belt.

I should’ve let Evan take me to see Dr. Carlyle. We’d already be home by now, but I couldn’t risk running into Jack again.

Now I’m paying the price with a kid to sew up my head.

“Let’s have a look.” The doctor tosses the clipboard onto the counter near Evan, finally catching sight of him. “Oh. Sorry, I didn’t see you there.”

"It's okay. Good things come to those who wait." Evan gives him a playful smirk.

Dr. Baylor, at least that's what is embroidered on his coat, smiles and gives Evan a once-over. "It's smart that you brought your wife in today."

Way to not be obvious, Doc.

"She's not my wife," Evan assures him.

Evan says he has the best gaydar in the world. He could pick a gay guy out of a crowd, and even though I didn't believe it at first, time after time, he has shown off his skills. Never in a million years would I have figured Dr. Baylor to be gay within the first thirty seconds of meeting him, but somehow, Evan did.

"Good to know." Dr. Baylor smiles at him again before finally directing his gaze at me, the patient in need of his attention. "What did you run into?"

"I'm not sure."

I'm too embarrassed to answer honestly because who runs into a giant parade float…? Me.

People do stupid things every day. I'm no different. Not all of them do it in quite the same manner I did or with as much public interest as I did it. It's my luck, though. When in doubt, find a large object and run straight into it.

"She ran into a parade float." Evan finds it too hysterical not to share, even at my expense.

I shoot a glare at him that wipes the playful smirk from his face.

"That takes skill."

"That's my girl," Evan says cheerfully and comes to stand next to me.

"May I?" Dr. Baylor asks, standing in front of me, with his white latex gloves ready to work their magic.

I nod and close my eyes as his fingers part my hair, exposing the reason I'm here. "Do I need stitches?"

"Looks like you'll need a few so it doesn't bust open and cause problems later."

I groan. I'm angry with myself. Only I would run right into a giant two-story float that is larger than most houses.

"You can lie back, and I'll get everything ready to stitch you up." Dr. Baylor rests his hand on my knees to stop me from denting the table underneath as my feet continue to move.

I hesitate long enough for Evan to say, "Girl, if you don't, I will."

"Shut up, Evan." I smile up at Dr. Baylor. "I'm sorry for his behavior."

His lips twitch. "No apologies needed."

When Dr. Baylor turns to leave, he and Evan give each other a look I can't quite describe before he walks out.

"That man is fine," Evan says as soon as the door closes.

"We're here for my head, not yours." I refrain from smacking his chest.

"Haven't you learned yet? It's always about me, Evie." Evan laughs as he stands and places his hands on my shoulders. "Don't blow this for me."

"How will I blow it? You do a pretty bang-up job of that on your own."

"Don't freak out."

"Evan, why don't you let him put a needle in your head and stay calm?"

"I can handle it. I'm a pretty tough guy." He keeps a straight face through his bullshit lie. "The man can poke me anywhere, and I wouldn't flinch."

"Um." I tilt my head, remembering him crying the last time he had a hangnail. "I remember…"

"Shh." He places his finger over my lips. "You have a head injury."

"So?" I mutter and narrow my gaze.

Our bickering is interrupted when Dr. Baylor returns with so many instruments that he needs a tray to carry them. "Here we go."

I close my eyes and bite my lip to stop the curses that are on the tip of my tongue.

Evan's hands grip my shoulders again. "Want me to hold your hand?"

Evan moves around to the side of the table opposite Dr. Baylor. "You don't mind, Doc, do you?"

"Not at all."

Drifting backward, I stare up at the ceiling and grab on to Evan's hand.

I glance at Dr. Baylor as he preps the instruments, but I avoid looking at the needles because I know I'll run out of here immediately. The sight of them terrifies me.

The doctor has a bit of bulk underneath his lab coat, which I assume is muscle, and his neck is thick, almost as wide as his head. His mouth is his best asset—perfect lips with the straightest white teeth I've ever seen. But the rest of him is rugged and right up Evan's alley.

Evan and Dr. Baylor are both handsome, just in different ways. Evan has a polish to him like he stepped out of the latest issue of *GQ*. His deep blue eyes, olive skin, and dark, wavy hair make him drop-dead gorgeous.

Dr. Baylor moves the instrument tray closer to me before I have a chance to look away. A glimpse of the needles and I tense.

"Close your eyes. It'll be quick," he promises.

I squeeze my eyes shut and grip Evan's hand so tightly that I probably cut off the circulation to his fingers. The prick of the numbing needle is the worst, and I wince through the entire thing, but I manage not to cry.

Instead of concentrating on the fact that he's about to sew up my head, I think about Jack and the moment I saw him and zone out.

He's the perfect distraction, even if thinking about him probably hurts worse than the stitches.

"Three stitches should do it." He snaps off the latex gloves, and I stare up at him in shock. "You may have some bleeding for the next few hours, but it should stop soon."

"That's it?" I practically made myself sick over the fact that I needed stitches, but somehow, it wasn't that bad.

"Yep. Here are instructions on how to care for the wound, and if you have any problems, feel free to come back, and I'll look at it for you."

I sit up and take a deep breath. "Thank you," I tell him, relieved it's over and ready to get out of here.

Evan pulls out a business card from his back pocket and hands it to Dr. Baylor. "Just in case you're ever in need of an evaluation." Evan's always using his work as a stockbroker to pick up men. It never ceases to amaze me how often it works too. But that's Evan. Balls bigger than his brain. "Call me anytime you need anything."

I swear he picks up a man everywhere we go. I don't know how he manages to do it, but I have to give him credit because he does it so effortlessly.

Dr. Baylor places the card in the front pocket of his coat with a giant smile. "I may just do that." Right on cue, he fishes a card out of his back pocket and hands it to Evan. "My cell is on the back in case you need to get physical." Dr. Baylor pounds on his chest, pretending he's choking. "I mean, need a physical."

"Uh-huh," I mutter under my breath. I shouldn't be shocked that someone has the same move as Evan, but somehow, I am.

Evan winks. "I may need a physical soon."

There's an awkward silence as they stare at each other. The sexual tension between them is thick, and I need to break this up before they go at one another.

I clear my throat to remind them I'm still in the room before hopping off the table.

"Sorry," Dr. Baylor says before finally walking out of the room.

"Are you done flirting?" I ask Evan with my hands on my hips, tapping my foot like a maniac.

"I think my work here is done." Evan's proud of himself and doesn't seem to care that it was at my expense. "You hungry?"

"Famished."

We walk through the back area of the urgent care, heading toward the door. Dr. Baylor looks up from his paperwork and smiles at Evan, who smiles back with a small wave.

"You two are making me nauseous."

Evan ignores my comment. "Moo and Oink?"

"Yep. Sounds good."

The name is silly, but they have the best food in town. Over the last few years, I've fallen in love with their burgers and fries. We usually go there so much that by the time our trip is over, I've increased my pants by a full size.

Twenty minutes later, we slide into a booth with our stomachs rumbling from the heavenly scent of fried pork, sizzling meat, and barbecue that surrounds us. I scan the restaurant and hide my face behind the menu because every person in the place is staring in our direction and whispering.

"Do I have something on my face?"

Evan glances up, and his eyes sweep across my face before they go back to the menu. "Nothing."

I lean across the table, letting my menu fall, and drop my voice to a whisper. "Then why the hell is everyone looking at me?"

"Probably because you're trending." There is a wicked glint in his eyes that makes me nervous.

I lurch backward. "I'm trending?"

"Yep. Trending."

"What does that even mean, Evan?" I ask through clenched teeth.

He grabs his phone and taps the screen a few times before shoving it in my face. "Trending with the hashtag #TogetherAgain."

I snatch the phone from his hand, and my mouth falls

open at what I see. Someone took a video as Jack tore his shirt off. He's standing over me, and the look on my face can't be confused with anything other than pure, unadulterated lust. He looks like a beast with his wide chest and golden skin glowing in the sunlight. "What the…"

Evan pulls the phone back with the biggest smile. "Yep, still sexy as fuck," he observes as he restarts the video.

"What can I get you two?" The waitress glances over Evan's shoulder to get a glimpse of the screen.

Evan holds the phone so she can get a better view of Jack and his Hulk-like move. "He's hot, right? It's not just me."

She leans forward, pulling her reading glasses down off her head. "I wouldn't kick him out of my bed. Would you?" She looks at Evan, who made it quite clear to Cornelia that he was gay after she asked him out last time we were in town.

Evan shakes his head and glances at me. "Um, never." He cocks his head like he's about to spill my secret. "She did, though."

I kick Evan underneath the table, and he flinches. Then I hide my face behind the menu, mortified.

Cornelia peers over the menu. "Girl, you need to have your head examined."

"Can I get the Moo and Oink burger with extra cheese?" I say.

I'm changing the subject. I'm not ready to discuss my love life with a stranger.

"Sure. What do you want, sugarplum?" she asks Evan with so much sweetness that my teeth almost ache.

"I'll take the special, sweetheart."

It takes everything in me not to gag at the cute little names they use for each other. Cornelia's a beautiful woman, though a good fifteen years Evan's senior, but that doesn't stop either of them from flirting shamelessly.

"Coming right up." She takes our menus, but I can't look her in the eyes or say anything until she's far enough away.

"Don't be such a shit in the pants, Evie. It's all in good fun."

I start to come back with a smart remark, only the door to the restaurant swings open, and my worst nightmare walks in—Myra Nelson in all her glory, and she's heading right toward me.

I grip the edges of the table, bracing myself for impact and trying not to move in hopes that she isn't about to make a scene.

"Hey, Evie. It's nice to see you." She stands over me with a hand resting on the back of the booth.

"Hey, Myra. How are you?"

Somehow, I've avoided everyone in the Nelson family during my few visits to Ridge Hollow over the years, but during this trip, I'm slowly checking them all off my list.

She turns to Evan, and her eyes sweep over him. "I'm pretty good. Who's the hunk?"

"Evan," he answers before I have a chance, extending his hand to her. "And you are?"

"Evan, this is Myra, Jack's sister," I inform him.

"I can see the resemblance."

"Are you two a thing?" Myra asks, getting right to the point.

"No, honey." Evan pats the empty space next to him, and Myra slides in without a second thought. "She doesn't have the parts that turn me on."

Her eyes roam over him, probably as shocked as I was the first time I heard the news. "You're way too hot to like dudes."

I roll my eyes, turning to face the window and tune them out as they chat. I watch the squirrels chasing each other up the tree just outside the window and pray Myra gets bored quickly and leaves. I'm in no mood for her shenanigans.

Hearing Jack's name draws my attention back to their conversation.

"Sorry, man. Jack is as straight as they come."

"Damn. A guy can always dream." Evan laughs. "Where is that sexy beast anyway?"

"He headed back to Philly for a few days."

I slide my gaze to Myra and Evan.

"So, when can I expect him back?" Evan waggles his eyebrows when he catches me looking in their direction.

"Soon," Myra says, drumming her hands on the table like we're boring her.

"Isn't that great news, Evie?"

"Yeah, sure." The vinyl of the booth squeaks as I squirm, and Myra turns her attention toward me.

Her fingers slow their movement, and she cocks her head, getting ready to pull the trigger on something shitty. "You know I never really liked you much, Evie."

This isn't news. Myra made it quite clear since the moment Jack and I started dating that she wasn't my biggest fan. She was just a little thing then, but she had so much hate in her heart and hadn't learned to filter.

"But I know Jack never got over you."

Her words are like a blow to the chest. *He never got over me?* Fuck, I never got over him…not the other way around.

"It's not like I went willingly."

"Well, you sure didn't come back."

Shutting down, I stare out the window, biting my tongue so as not to say something I'll regret. Myra is Jack's sister, but as much as he hurt me, I won't take it out on her. Instead, I twist my hands in my lap, thinking about Jack and how things could've been so different if I'd stayed.

Evan must sense my unease, and he takes pity on me, striking up a conversation with her about her favorite topic—herself.

"Jack, where were you? I waited as long as I could," I ask over the phone.

"I'll give you one guess." His tone tells me it has something to do with his sister.

I know he would never stand me up on purpose. I just hated not knowing where he was or if something bad had happened. I knew it wasn't like Jack not to tell me he wasn't going to make it.

"Myra?"

"She broke the faucet just as I was walking out the door. My mother started screaming when water started spraying everywhere." He sucks in a deep breath. "I had to shut off the water, and I need to fix the leak before I can leave. I'm so sorry, Evie. Will you forgive me?"

"Always, Jack."

"Love you, Evie girl."

"Love you too."

Myra has hated me since I became Jack's girlfriend. Maybe she thinks I am trying to steal her big brother from her. I wish I could make her see that in me she's gaining a friend, and someday, when I marry Jack, a sister.

JACK

"How long are you going to be gone?" Cameron's standing in the doorway of my office with his arms crossed.

I rifle through a few contracts that have landed on my desk over the weekend, not bothering to look up. "A week, maybe more. I have something important to take care of."

"Does this have anything to do with the girl in the video?"

I lean back in my chair, resting my elbows on the armrests and stare at him. "Maybe."

Cameron's smile morphs into his typical cocky smirk. "Never thought I'd see the day when you'd chase a girl."

"She's not any girl, Cam. She's my girl."

He looks at me funny because in all the time we've known each other, I've never claimed anyone as mine. In no way, shape, or form have I ever been a one-woman kind of guy since I met Cameron at Penn State.

He pushes off the doorway and walks into my office,

studying me like a zoo animal. “She must be something if she has you by the short hairs.”

“No one has me by anything, asshat. And for your information, Evie is the only girl I’ve ever loved.”

He makes a gagging sound before pretending to throw up in the trash across the room. Cameron collapses on the couch opposite my desk and throws his arm over his face. “It’s been boring here without you, bro.”

“Come with me,” I urge him, but I know he won’t go. Someone has to run the day-to-day operations of Dirty Deeds Designs, the company I started in college as a project in my business classes.

By the start of senior year, I’d secured loans and officially launched Dirty Deed Designs—an online apparel company. I didn’t have a graphics background, but Cameron did, and he jumped in as soon as I told him about the idea. I handled the advertising, merchandising, along with modeling our gear. Cameron handled everything else. Within the first year, we tripled our projected profits and have only grown from there.

“Nah. I’ll hold down the fort while you chase the skirt.” He grins.

“I’m going to catch her, Cam. Mark my words.”

“When you want something, you get it. I’ve yet to see you fail.”

“It’s not going to be easy,” I admit. The way things ended between us wasn’t good, and if her reaction to seeing me yesterday is any indication of how she feels about me now, I’m going to have to work hard to get her back.

Cameron sighs loudly before climbing to his feet. “Nothing that’s worth a shit ever is. Right?”

“That’s the truth,” I agree with him, following him with my eyes as he heads toward the door.

“I know you’re in a rush, so just text me and keep me in the loop.”

“Will do.”

He slaps my door and yells “Pussy whipped” over his shoulder before disappearing into his office. I can still hear him snickering as he shuts his door.

“Still an asshat!” I yell back before burying my nose in the final stack of papers that calls for my attention.

Once all the paperwork is signed and I’ve finished everything that’s important, I gather up my laptop, keys, and phone and head to my condo loft next door to grab a bag of clothes.

I’m going back to where my past is my future.

“What do you think it’ll be like?” Evie asks as we stare up at the stars. We’ve been lying next to each other in the tall, thick summer grass for hours.

I stare at her profile in the moonlight. She’s beautiful, just like the day I first laid eyes on her in eighth-grade homeroom. “What?”

She turns to me and smiles. “Being an adult.”

My hand drifts across the blades of grass and covers hers, intertwining our fingers. “It’s going to be amazing.”

She turns back to the sky and gives my hand a light squeeze. “I can’t wait to be together always.”

“Me too, Evie, me too.” I smile to myself, envisioning our future.

"Do you see that?" She points upward, hoping I'll look, but I can't take my eyes off her.

"Yes." I inch closer, needing to feel her body next to mine.

"That's Polaris," she whispers. "It's always the brightest star in the sky and barely ever moves. If we're ever apart, just look up and know I'm looking at it too."

Our shoulders are touching, and my heart's thumping uncontrollably. "Are you going somewhere, Evie?" I hold my breath, waiting for her to reply.

"No, Jack." She glances in my direction.

I blow out a shaky breath. "You scared me."

"We're officially freshmen," she whispers and bites her bottom lip, the same one I want to kiss.

I need to kiss Evie. I've waited nine months for this moment. Evie and I have been an item for two months, but I've never given her more than a peck because she'd never open-mouth kissed someone before. In truth, neither have I, but I've wanted to experience it with her since the day she became mine. Evie had told me that she was scared. I've been patiently waiting for her to be ready.

Rolling to my side, pressing my body against hers, I push her hands over her head. "Evie," I whisper, hovering above her and staring into her eyes. "I need to kiss you."

"Okay," she says softly.

I lower my face to hers and hold my breath before pressing my lips to her sweet mouth. Tiny sparks shoot through my body, igniting a fire I've never felt before. The ridges of her bottom lip feel like mountains as I sweep my tongue across them. Her lips part just enough that the tip of her tongue meets mine, and I'm unable to stop the moan that escapes from my throat.

My free hand glides across her cheek, coming to a rest on her neck, just above her feverish pulse. Scooting closer, leaving no space between us—my front to her side—I curl my fingers around the back of her neck and nudge her lips farther apart with my tongue. The ecstasy of her mouth as my tongue presses forward, skating across hers, is something I've never experienced before.

The sweetness. The softness. I don't just feel the kiss against my mouth, but all over my body. I'm drunk on Evie, and I don't think life will ever be the same again.

I pull away and gasp for air, feeling light-headed. "That was…"

"Amazing," she finishes my sentence.

"I don't want to leave here," I whisper.

"We don't have to go."

I close my eyes, wishing I could stay in this moment forever. "Your dad will never let me see you again if I bring you home late, Evie."

"Just one more kiss," she says with a smile.

"Anything you want." I give her hand a tight squeeze and kiss her with more force this time, knowing she wants it as badly as I do.

Time seems to stop, the crickets in the field quieting to a whisper as if they know this moment is magical.

Evie Bailey officially owns me, and she always will.

I can't imagine ever kissing anyone else.

EVIE

The sun's hanging low in the sky, dancing over the two-story skyline of Ridge Hollow's downtown as Evan and I window-shop. It's picture-perfect with its quaintness and old country charm.

Evan leads me across the street even though I told him I am ready to call it a day. We've spent so much time in the tiny square that we practically have the stores memorized. However, my heart isn't into shopping. I haven't been able to get Jack out of my head since the moment our eyes locked.

I was stupid.

I shouldn't have run from him, but it was the only thing that felt right. It was fight or flight, and I didn't want to make a scene. I have a lump the size of a golf ball to prove exactly how stupid it was, but there's no do-overs.

Evan wraps his arm around my shoulder and pulls me to his side. "I could stay here forever."

"You'd miss the city too much if we left." I drop my

head to his shoulder. Evan loves the city and the nightlife it provides.

I never imagined leaving this little town when I was young, but I didn't have a choice. I thought Ridge Hollow would always be my home. Every time Evan and I come back here, it gets harder to leave, but this time, it may be impossible after seeing Jack.

"Oh. My. God! It's finally open." He stares at a window full of cupcakes and pies with nothing but lust in his eyes. He's been waiting for them to open since we got to town a few days ago.

Evan's always had an insatiable sweet tooth. He'd probably trade our friendship for a lifetime supply of his favorite treat—red velvet cupcakes with cream cheese frosting.

"We have to go in there. I'm starving." He pulls me toward the entrance with him when I don't move.

"You're always starving." I roll my eyes, but I let him drag me inside because, well, it's cupcakes, and I know better than to get between Evan and his sweets. He is a walking poster child for that candy bar commercial where the people are grumpy until they get their chocolate fix.

As soon as we enter the tiny shop, I'm immediately high on the sugary sweetness of the air. One by one, the different scents hit me—chocolate, vanilla, strawberry, and my favorite…caramel.

There isn't a thing in the display case that I don't want to devour, and every ounce of it will hang over the top of my jeans if I'm not careful.

I'm petite, and even the slightest weight gain makes every inch of my body go out of whack. Evan will never understand this since he has a metabolism that allows him to eat anything he wants without the risk of gaining a pound.

He's never had to worry about fitting into his clothes. *The bastard*. Sometimes I hate him for it, but most of all, I'm jealous as hell. He eats without abandon and doesn't seem to pay a price for it. He's still as trim as the day I met him, while I'm a little fluffier than I was in my teens. I blame Evan and his obsession with tasty treats.

"Evan, I'm going to gain ten pounds just smelling the sweets in this place."

"I'm sure Jack won't care," he says quickly, but he doesn't dare look at me because he knows that his comment hits a nerve.

"I don't care about Jack," I respond flippantly.

I'm lying and defensive.

Jack Nelson is all I can think about. The fact that my head is still throbbing from where it hit the float doesn't help. It's a constant reminder of our encounter.

Evan glances over his shoulder before humming an annoying response that I pretend not to hear before his gaze locks on the third row of cupcakes that look more like tiny masterpieces than dessert. "Ooh, I'm going to max out my credit card in here. How many turtle cupcakes do you need to drown your sorrows tonight, Evie?"

Tapping my fingernail against my chin, I stare at the gooey goodness of the turtle cupcakes. One isn't enough, but three may be pushing it. They look so tempting with all the caramel oozing off the sides in thick ribbons, pooling on the tray below them, that I can't stop myself. "Two."

"Can I help you?" the lady behind the counter asks,

and she stares at me for a few seconds before gasping. “Evie?”

I blink twice, wondering if I’m seeing who I think I am. “Renee?”

“OMG!” she screeches in her annoying, high-pitched tone that nearly bursts my eardrums.

Suddenly, the cupcakes don’t seem so appealing when putting up with her bullshit is the price I’d have to pay to sink my teeth into their deliciousness.

Renee and I were best friends. We were almost inseparable at times. Once I began dating Jack and she hooked up with Jess, things between us were never the same.

“You look great,” I lie because she looks like absolute shit, but I’m too nice to say it. The dark circles under her eyes are enormous.

The girl I knew in high school is gone and has been replaced by a woman who appears a good ten years older than me. Time hasn’t been on her side. Her cheeks are fuller, the shade of her makeup doesn’t suit her skin tone at all, giving her an orange glow like she has spent too much time in the tanning bed and uses too much bronzer. The pink T-shirt embroidered with a giant cupcake does nothing to make her look any younger either.

Renee is far removed from the slender girl I was friends with years ago. Wide hips and thick thighs have replaced her previously slim figure that she always flaunted.

“Thanks,” she says, her cheeks turning a rosy shade of pink. “So do you.”

Evan clears his throat as if I could forget his company so easily. The man gets attention no matter where he goes.

“Sorry. Evan, this is Renee, my best friend from school. Renee, this is Evan, my best friend today.”

I cringe inwardly at how bitchy that sounds, but it’s not my intent…or maybe it is. It doesn’t matter either way because I stopped caring about Renee a long time ago.

Evan shoots her his killer smile, the one that could drop the panties of most females if he weren’t so into peen. “It’s nice to meet you, Renee.”

Her blush deepens as his dazzling smile works its magic. Sometimes I think Evan could turn even the straightest of men with his charm and wit.

“It’s completely my pleasure. We should do coffee,” Renee suggests with hopeful eyes as she slides on a pair of plastic gloves. “We need to catch up when I’m not working. I just landed this job this month and I barely get a day off, but I’ll make time for you.”

That will never happen. I’m trying to think of a reply that won’t sound as harsh as, *“Thanks, but no thanks.”*

“That would be great. She’d love that,” Evan answers for me.

“But you have to come too, Evan.” Renee smiles brightly, the flush on her cheeks spreading down her neck.

“Of course. I’ll be there, darlin’,” he coos at her, making my insides churn.

Where his country drawl came from, I have no idea, but he nails it.

“Oh my God. It’s going to be like old times.” She’s practically squealing with delight and clapping her plastic gloves together, making the most hideous noise.

“Fabulous.” The bitchiness in my voice is hidden by

the chatter of kids filling the shop; they are coming through the door in droves.

I'll get him back for this, even though he has no idea about Renee and her bullshit. She's the last person I want to invite back into my life, yet he's opened the door and rolled out the red carpet for her.

"Softball practice must be over. I'd better hurry. So, what can I get you two?"

Evan places our order and pays while I stand off to the side so the kids can ogle the cupcake display.

Thank God for the bakery case between us or I'd have to hug her and talk longer than necessary. I've had too many ghosts from my past in the last few days to be forced into dealing with yet another awkward exchange.

"Bye. I hope I will see you soon, Evan. You too, Evie." Renee waves at us as we walk toward the door.

Evan shoves a cupcake in his mouth as we step outside. "She seems nice." Crumbs fall from his bottom lip as he pushes the rest inside.

I glare at him with my hands on my hips, trying not to entirely lose my shit. He deserves a little attitude for his overly friendly display with Renee.

"Evan," I sigh, but I can't be mad at him. Not when he has frosting and crumbs all over his face.

"What?" He looks so innocent and bewildered it's almost cute.

"Renee isn't a good person," I tell him as I wipe away the messy bits of cupcake. "She's not the kind of friend you'd want. Trust me on this. She's bad news."

He makes a sour face. "Seriously? She seems really sweet."

"Dead. Fucking. Serious."

"Come on." He nudges me playfully with his elbow, but I don't move.

I narrow my eyes on him instead, driving my point home. He has to know I won't budge on this. I won't welcome her back into my life. I can't do it. I won't.

"Whatever you want. If you hate her, I'll hate her."

I've never hated anyone before, not even Renee. I simply don't have room for her in my life again.

"Maybe she's changed. We all do in time," he says.

I know he's right, but sometimes change isn't enough to make up for all the bad of the complicated past we share.

"Who's this?" I ask Renee as we get to the diner to meet Jess. There's a guy with him I have never seen before.

Jack was supposed to come with me, but he had to watch his little sister. And after the stunt she pulled the last time he brought her along, he decided they would stay home. I offered to go to his house, but my dad is already on my ass about how much time I spend with Jack.

"I'm Kevin, Jess's cousin," he introduces himself and extends his hand to me to shake.

"Nice to meet you." I give him a weak smile. Renee didn't say anything about Jess bringing anyone with him. Maybe she didn't know.

I don't think Jack would get mad at me, but I am sure he would have liked to have known there was going to be another guy here.

I follow them inside and slide into the booth, expecting Renee to sit next to me, but she scoots in with Jess, leaving this Kevin guy to take up the empty spot on my bench.

I edge close to the window, as far away from him as I can, trying not to be obvious. This guy, Kevin, is draping his arm behind me on the back of the cushioned booth, and it almost makes it feel like he believes this is a double date. Which it definitely is not. I'm with Jack, and I don't want anyone else.

Not now.

Not ever.

"Do you live around here?" I ask, attempting to be friendly while we wait for the waitress to come over and take our order.

"Just visiting. You know, Evie, was it?"

I nod.

"You're even prettier than Jess said."

"Um, thanks, I guess." I scowl at Renee as she giggles. "I need to go to the bathroom. Excuse me." I can feel Kevin's eyes raking over my body as I get up from my seat. He doesn't give me much room, forcing me to rub against him.

"Renee, would you come with me?" I say with a forced smile, trying to be cordial and not lose my shit.

"I guess. Be right back, baby." She practically shoves her tongue down Jess's throat before following me.

When we get into the bathroom, I corner her. "What is that?" I throw my hand toward the door.

"What? Kevin. Pfft. He's nice, and you have to admit he's cute. Jack couldn't come, so..." She shrugs indifferently as though she is innocent in all this.

No one could ever be a stand-in for Jack. How could she do this to me?

"You know Jack wouldn't like this. Why would you think this is okay? Kevin thinks we are on a date."

Renee goes to the sink and stares at me in the mirror as she applies fresh lip gloss after smearing the layer she was wearing all over Jess's lips. "Calm down. You're not married to Jack, and it isn't like you have to do anything with Kevin. That is, if you don't want to." She winks.

"I'm going home." I start for the door when she grabs my hand.

"I'm sorry. Don't leave. Jess will get mad at me. Please, just eat with us, and I promise I will tell Jack you had no idea Kevin was coming."

"I don't know, Renee. You know Jess would flip out if I did this to you."

She pouts. "Come on, Evie. It won't be so bad. I'll even make sure Jess pays for your food."

"It's not about that, Renee. I have a boyfriend."

"We can take Jack a milk shake after, and you can tell him that Kevin tagged along. It's no big deal. It's not like you are on a date with the guy."

"He seems to think otherwise."

"So let him think it. What's it going to hurt? His girlfriend dumped him. Jess feels bad for him. Rachel was supposed to come, and we were gonna make this a group thing. But then Jack couldn't come, and Rachel flaked on us."

"It makes me uncomfortable."

"Seriously, Evie. I don't get why you are making such a big deal out of this. It isn't like you are doing anything wrong. You're just hanging out with me."

I know she is right, but that doesn't mean other people

won't think I'm on a date with this guy. What if someone tells Jack before I get the chance to?

When we go back to the table, Jack is standing in front of the table with Myra.

Great.

"I changed my mind," Jack says with a tight smile when I walk up to him.

I grab his worn T-shirt and wrap my fingers around the soft material, pressing my body against his. "I was just about to order to-go and go home."

Jack pulls me into his side and kisses my forehead as he glares at Kevin. "No need to leave, Evie girl. I'm here now." Jack's eyes still haven't left Kevin's. "Mind moving so I can sit by my girl?"

He emphasizes the word "my" with a slight growl. Kevin moves without saying a word, but it doesn't make anything more comfortable. Kevin, Renee, and Jess sit on the other side of the table as Myra, Jack, and I settle in across from them.

Jack places his arm around my shoulder, and it never leaves. I know he's not mad, but we probably won't be hanging out with Renee and Jess for a very long time.

JACK

Around noon, I finally finish my cup of coffee and head toward the barn. I trudge through the thick, overgrown grass behind the house and wonder why Myra isn't taking better care of the place.

"Ma!"

"In here," she yells from inside.

I push open the door to find my mother sitting in the middle of the barn on an upside-down bucket. "What are you doing?"

Brushing a few strands of gray hair away from her face with the back of her glove-covered hand, she glances up at me. "Just a little spring cleaning."

I rub the back of my neck and blow out a quick breath as I peer around. This is more than spring cleaning. The barn is a mess and looks like it's sat untouched for more than one winter.

"Where should I start?"

“I don’t know.” She runs her hands back and forth across her jeans and glances around before she shrugs. “Upstairs, maybe. I haven’t been up there in years.”

I look toward the loft, the place Evie and I would sneak off to when we wanted to be alone. “I’ll clean it out, Ma. You just relax a little.”

I test out the wooden ladder before I start to climb, making sure it can handle my weight without crumbling into a thousand pieces and taking me with it. I assume it hasn’t been used since the last time I was up here and could very easily send my ass straight to the ground.

When I reach the landing, I shake my head in disbelief. The upstairs is worse than I ever could’ve imagined. The years of neglect are evident as I look around. “Stand clear of the center. I’m just going to throw stuff down.”

“Be careful up there. I’m heading to the house to stay out of your way.”

I start with the easy stuff that’s scattered around the floor, throwing it over the railing. There’s satisfaction as each forgotten item hits the dirt floor below with a loud thump.

When I yank an old, tattered bale of hay off the top of the pile, I uncover something I haven’t seen in six years. I stand there, staring at it.

"Jack." Evie sits cross-legged facing the wall, drawing a red heart. "Do you promise I'll always be yours?"

I'm stretched out on my side with my head propped in my palm, taking in the beauty of her naked body against the stark white barn wall. "You'll always be my girl, Evie. I'm going to marry you someday," I promise.

She scribbles her name over the heart, adding my name too before turning to me with a heartfelt smile. "This will always be here to remind you of that promise."

Pushing myself up, I take the marker from her, adding "4-EVER" underneath our names. "I don't need a reminder to know I love you, Evie Bailey." Throwing the pen over my shoulder, I haul her into my lap before holding her cheeks in my hands. "Nothing will ever separate us. Nothing."

"You promise?"

"I promise," I say against her lips before pressing my mouth to hers, quieting her doubt. There's only one girl in the world for me, and it's her.

She wraps her legs around me, lowering her body

slowly onto my hardness. I snake my arms around her waist, holding her body against mine, and we rock together in the sweetest rhythm. I bury my face in her blond hair and moan in sated bliss.

"I love you," I whisper into her ear.

"Forever and ever," she murmurs back.

"Jack." My mom's voice pulls me out of the memory.

"Yeah?"

"You okay up there?"

I blink a few times. I don't know how long I've been transfixed by my memory of the day Evie drew on the barn wall, permanently declaring our love. The black marker I used to scratch away the drawing Evie made had faded, unlike the image underneath. I turn my back to the memento.

"I'm fine. Don't worry about me."

"I didn't hear you moving. Thought maybe you passed out from the heat. Want some lemonade when I head in?"

"Sure," I tell her before the barn goes silent again.

I keep throwing the old shit over the railing, but my thoughts remain on the image and our past.

"Where did you tell your parents you were sleeping tonight?" I cocoon us in a fuzzy blanket I stole from my mom's linen closet to protect us from the hay strewn across the loft floor.

"I told them I was staying with Cindy's family for the night." Her finger traces tiny hearts across my chest, leaving a thin red mark where her fingernail has pressed.

My hand tangles in her silky hair as I weave it around my fingers. "What if they show up there?"

"They're not home." She glances up with a smirk. "They actually went camping, so I figured it was the perfect cover."

I pull her body closer to mine. "I can't believe I have you for the entire night."

"Someday we won't have to sneak around, Jack."

Staring at the heart she's just drawn on the wall, I kiss her forehead and smile. "I can't wait to have you all to myself."

"Forever and ever."

"Love you, Evie girl," I say to her as she drifts off to sleep in my arms.

"Lemonade's here," Ma announces as she walks inside, startling me.

I climb down the rickety old ladder, and she's waiting for me with a tray of cookies and an entire pitcher of ice-cold homemade lemonade.

We're halfway done with our first glass when Myra finally makes her grand entrance. I'm pissed she slept in, and from the looks of the barn, she hasn't been helping out at all.

She plops down next to me and grabs a cookie off the tray. "Good morning, family."

I give her a sideways glance. "Finally awake, princess?"

"Barely." She takes a bite of the cookie and flips her hair over her shoulder.

I tighten my fist, trying to control my aggravation with my little sister, but I can't contain my frustration. "What the hell, Myra? Why haven't you been helping Ma?"

Bored by my little speech, she picks at her jet-black fingernail polish and flicks the chips toward me. "I don't do manual labor, Jack. In case you haven't noticed, I'm a woman now."

"So is Ma, but you don't see her sitting on her ass."

"It's fine," Ma deflects and waves off my comment.

"This is bullshit." Myra shouldn't be allowed to pull the woman card out when it suits her. A little hard work never hurt anybody, especially a goddamn teenager. "Don't let her off the hook that easy. She gets away with way too much."

"Farm life isn't for everyone," Myra says and narrows her eyes, knowing damn well I'm about to pop my lid. "Cranky because of Evie?" She pushes my buttons because no one knows them better than a little sister.

"No," I say a little too quickly.

She went there. I shouldn't be surprised. Myra has always been wicked. If you'd hit her, she'd knock your ass down out of spite. If she had been born a boy, the entire world would have been in trouble.

"Mm-hmm. I saw her yesterday after you left." Her fingers brush at the corner of her mouth, wiping away stray crumbs. The shit-eating grin she flashes over the brim of her lemonade doesn't go unnoticed by me like it does Ma.

She's taunting me, trying to get me off the subject of her laziness. She's a pro, but I don't take the bait. "Doesn't matter. Go change your clothes, and get your ass out here to help." I push her legs, forcing her body off the crate.

Myra flips me off before she walks out, heading

toward the main house. Skipping away, she's singing, "Jack and Evie sitting in a tree."

This is going to be a long day. I guzzle down the rest of the lemonade before I head back to the loft to throw some more old shit around and blow off a little steam.

"Jack! Wait up." Jason starts to jog in my direction. He's wearing a pale yellow dress shirt and brown tie, looking every bit the high school counselor.

We'd been best friends since kindergarten, but we drifted apart after I went away to Penn State and he enrolled at UCLA.

It was like he fell off the face of the earth and vanished for years. I found out a few months ago that he came back to Ridge Hollow and was hired at the high school as a counselor.

"What's up, bud?" I stop near the entrance to the general store and wait for him. "I was just about to text you to grab a beer."

"I saw the video," he says, trying to catch his breath.

"Fuck," I groan. I scrub my hands down my face. The entire town has seen the video by now. "Don't start."

"Did it blow your mind seeing her again?" His forest-green eyes are glittering with excitement.

"I don't know how I feel," I confide in him.

Jason knows everything about Evie. He was by my side during the entire relationship, and he made me get back out there after it ended. He refused to let me wallow in self-pity and sadness when Evie broke my heart.

"Want to get a drink and talk about it?"

"You mean drown my emotions at the bottom of a bottle?"

It wouldn't help a damn thing, but after the last few days, I could use a drink to mask some of the pain. The absence of Evie in my life is heavy on my mind and heart.

"Yep. Why the hell not?"

"Sounds like the perfect way to spend a night."

"I'll meet you at the Rusty Nail later. I have to grab a few things and drop them off for my mom."

"I'll see you there, man."

Jason walks back to the other side of the street, and I'm not even in the general store thirty seconds when Mrs. Griffin starts yapping. "I saw Evie today."

"Yeah." I'm trying to play it cool. I wander toward the back of the store and out of the watchful and nosy eyes of Mrs. Griffin.

She's always been a busybody. It doesn't help that she runs the general store either. If you need medicine, she knows what ails you. If you need birth control, she knows you're getting laid. If you buy a pregnancy test, you better not even try to keep it a secret. Besides being the owner, she is the town gossip. They go hand in hand and have always annoyed the hell out of me.

"You need any help back there?" Mrs. Griffin yells across the store.

"I got it." I grab the last item on my mom's list. "Nosy bitch," I mutter under my breath.

"What was that?"

"Nothing," I snap louder than intended.

If I passed Mrs. Griffin on the street without knowing her, I'd think she was the sweetest old lady. Her curly gray hair and funky red glasses partnered with her polka-dot dresses make her look a tad eccentric, but completely harmless.

But to know her…is to hate her.

I head straight to the register, ready to get out of here before Mrs. Griffin sticks her nose where it doesn't belong again. I'm ready for her shit-talking as I unload the ten or so items I grabbed.

She reads each price sticker aloud as she uses one finger to punch in the numbers on her archaic cash register. She slowly lowers each item in the bag, looking at me from under her lashes as she reaches for the next. "So, what have you been up to? It's been years since you've stayed this long."

"Just visiting my mom and sister," I answer, knowing she already knows why I am here. I run my hand over my head and let out a sigh, eager to get the hell out of here.

The bitch knows everything about every-damn-body in this town. She's made it her life's mission. She probably knows what I had for dinner last night too.

The lines around her lips become more visible when she purses them. "Is something wrong?"

"No, Mrs. Griffin." My teeth are clenched tightly together as I try to avoid shooting off at the mouth. She'd be on the phone to my mom before my ass even walked out the door if I did.

"Keep the change," I tell her, tossing a fifty on the counter before grabbing the bag and leaving. That woman is insufferable. I don't think anyone truly likes her.

"Jack?"

The sound of that voice makes my body recoil; she grates on my nerves. Even after all these years, her voice is worse than fingernails on a chalkboard. I turn to face her, and I'm shocked that she doesn't look anything like the girl I knew in high school. "Renee?"

Her eyes travel up my body slowly, too slowly for my liking. "Damn," she says before whistling. "What happened to you? You're all big and shit." She reaches out, wrapping her hand around my bicep.

"I work out." I start to inch backward because I have nothing to say to her. I have never liked her. Evie was always best friends with her, and I never could understand why.

"I might need a good workout soon too. Maybe you can help me." She winks.

It takes everything in me not to gag. "I won't be around for that long," I lie. I should tell her that her ass could use a lot of miles on the treadmill, but I refrain. Knowing her, she would try to take it as me flirting with her.

"That's a shame." Her eyes sweep across my shoulders. "You look like you could give me a real good workout."

She's still as classless and rude as she was back in high school. "It was nice to see you again, Renee," I spit out, being kinder than she deserves.

"Did you see Evie?" she asks before I have a chance to turn my back, but she already knows the answer. She wouldn't ask unless she knew. That's the type of person she is…an asshole.

"I did."

She steps closer, glancing around before whispering, "Are you mad at her?"

"No," I deadpan, ready for this conversation to be over. I don't want to discuss Evie with her. I don't want to speak to her at all.

"I would be if I were you. I mean, if she…"

Her words knock me back. What would I have to be mad at Evie about? Besides the obvious that she moved away, and time and distance tore us apart. Renee's trying to imply that there was something more, but I'm not taking the bait.

"Jack? Dude, is that you?" Jess walks up from behind Renee, fifty pounds heavier with a full beard, wearing the ugliest flannel shirt I've ever seen. My favorite part of the new Jess look is his mullet that fits him to a T.

"Jess?"

"Hell yeah." He holds out his hand, wearing the biggest smile. "Dude."

"Look at you," I say while I shake his hand, because I don't know what else to say to him. I never liked him all that much, but I always felt a bit sorry for him because he was so into Renee. Looks like some things never change.

"Yeah, and look at you too."

He wraps his arm around Renee's shoulder. "We're still together after all these years." He smirks when Renee places her hand on his stomach and snuggles against him, putting on a full display of gag-reflex-inducing affection. "Tied the knot and everything." He says it like he is so proud. Renee damn sure isn't any prize.

He made sure to get the dig in about still being together since Evie and I are not. It was always a competition with us, and they have clearly won.

How the hell am I supposed to respond to that kind of an asshole statement?

Good job, man. Way to go.

I say nothing, hoping they will move on.

"Hey." Jess glances down at Renee and back at me. "We should have Jack over for dinner while he's in town. We could catch up. It's been way too long."

I'm thinking it hasn't been long enough, but I don't tell him that.

"That's a great idea, honey." Renee smiles at me. "We'd love to have you."

There's no way in hell I'm going to their house. I don't need to be reminded how they survived while Evie and I crumbled to pieces. "Yeah. Maybe sometime next week. I gotta run, though."

"Tell your mom hi," Jess says, pulling Renee closer.

"Sure," I call over my shoulder with no intentions of mentioning it.

"Fuckin' Jack Nelson. Can you believe it, baby?"

"He looks so different," she says to him before I can get far enough away not to overhear their conversation.

"Yeah, but I bet he isn't as happy as us." He chuckles.

"Asshats," I mumble to myself before tossing the bag in my truck. I should have guessed those two would stick it out and never leave this place. Who else would have either of them?

Growing up, Evie and I always called the town Sleepy Hollow and dreamed of moving away. I wasn't willing to spend eternity surrounded by the same ten stores, one main road, and a bunch of town gossips like Mrs. Griffin without Evie at my side. I wanted more. Without Evie, there was nothing here for me. I had no reason to stay.

But now, she's back, and so am I.

EVIE

"Are you ready to go to the cemetery?" Evan asks while checking his email as I pour myself a cup of coffee.

"We'll go later before they close."

"Evie," he warns.

"Don't start with me, Evan. It's been a trying couple of days. I need to do something first."

I need to do anything but what I came here for.

I don't know if I'll ever be ready to go back there, but I know I have to go to the cemetery and have my father's ashes placed next to my mother's.

We've been in town a week, and I've put it off every time he asks. I haven't been able to find the courage or the strength to go, even with his constant pestering.

It's too hard.

It stirs up too much pain.

It brings back a time in my life I wish I could forget,

but I can't. I'm marked by it. What happened shaped me and changed who I was and made me who I am now.

"I won't let you forget."

As if I need a reminder.

I sigh loudly just like Evan usually does. "I know. It'll get done today."

I wish he'd drop it. I'll do it when I'm ready, which may be never.

"If we're not there by three, I'm dragging you there by that beautiful blond hair of yours."

I stick out my tongue at him. He's so damn bossy sometimes, even when it's for my own good. He knows I'm dreading going there. He knows what it means to me, and it never gets any easier.

"I feel like a hike. Want to come?" I ask, trying to change the subject.

"Sure. I'd love to."

I gawk at him, blinking a few times. Evan hates the outdoors. He's more of the sit in a bar and look pretty type. "You really want to come?"

"I think I need to stay close to you today."

I blink again and cross my arms over my chest. "Why?"

He shrugs and sets down his cappuccino. "Figure I'll get into trouble otherwise."

"You always cause trouble." I laugh softly.

"If you don't want me to come, I can probably go hang out with *Renee* today." His expression is so serious I want to punch him.

"Don't you dare."

He gives me a mischievous smile, but I know he's only joking. "I think Renee and I could be BFFs."

The happiness fades from my face, and my stare hardens. "Shut up." I glare at him. "It's me or her, buddy."

"Fine. If I have to choose…" He takes a drink.

"Ugh!"

I stand from the table, needing some fresh air. The sunshine outside is calling my name, and the last thing I want to do today is stay cooped up in the rental we've secured for thirty days. "I'm leaving in five minutes."

"I'm ready to go when you are," he tells me as he walks over to the sink and puts his mug in it.

I run upstairs to change into a pair of spandex capris and a sports bra before pulling on a hoodie. Then I grab my tennis shoes, jamming my feet inside without undoing the laces.

Evan's waiting for me on the front porch when I make my way downstairs. I push open the front door and finish pulling my hair into a messy bun.

"Ready?" I ask him when I'm done fussing with my hair.

"Where are we headed?"

"A special place."

He quirks an eyebrow. "A Jack place?"

I jog down the front steps, unable to look him in the eyes. "Maybe. Just get your ass moving, Evan."

I know what he's thinking, and he's right. I'm still in love with Jack Nelson. After seeing him, he's all I can think about. If I'm honest with myself, he's all I want. But I can't have him.

Evan walks quickly to keep up with me, tucking his hands into the front pockets of his skinny jeans. The man can't dress down even for a hike. He must always remain in style in case he runs into someone. There aren't many people for him to run into in Ridge Hollow, but it doesn't stop him from being prepared. The man always appears flawless. I should despise him for it, really, but I adore him even when he's giving me shit and looks good while doing it.

I'm nervous as we walk; it's been so long since I've been here. I replay the day Jack and I walked here for the first time in my mind with every step. I remember the way he grabbed my hand after school. I could tell he was nervous. I was too. Jack always had a way of making me feel as though butterflies were fluttering in my chest. The boy did crazy things to my pulse.

He still has that effect on me.

When we come to the clearing, it takes my breath away just like it did years ago. The trees have grown taller, but everything else is just as I remember it. Everything here screams Jack. He always loved it here.

"It's a lake." Evan's voice is so childlike as he stares ahead in wonderment.

I gaze at the water, remembering every time I'd been here with Jack. "It's special."

I can almost see the ghosts of our youth walking past me, holding hands as we had many times. My vision blurs. One blink and tears cascade down my face and plop near my feet, falling like raindrops against the blades of grass.

I walk toward the edge, near the very spot I stood with Jack, and sit down in the grass, pulling my knees close against my chest. I miss how innocent and in love we were back then. We were in such a hurry to grow up. Things were so easy when we were younger. Now look at us. We are as complicated as it comes.

Evan sits next to me, stretching out and leaning back on his hands. "It's really beautiful, Evie, but why's it so significant?"

I stare across the lake, my eyes sweeping back and forth over the tree line with the first buds of spring starting to blossom into flowers. "It's where I first became his, Evan. This place belonged to Jack and me."

My heart races when he asks me if I've ever been kissed. In this moment, I know Jack is going to press his lips to mine, and I'll never be the same. This will change everything, but I am so ready for it to happen.

"No," I say softly as my cheeks heat.

"Me either. Don't worry. We'll figure it out."

I hold my breath as we both lean forward, moving closer to become each other's first. I would be more nervous if he had kissed someone before, but just like me, he's a novice. Whether or not we are doing it right doesn't matter—we have nothing to compare it to. There is only this, and it feels right, natural.

When his lips finally touch mine, I feel a tingle down my body that emanates from my lips. His breathing is ragged as his hand tangles in my hair, and his other arm snakes around my back. I close my eyes, overcome by so much emotion I can't bear to stare into his any longer. My fingers creep under the side of his shirt, feeling the softness of his skin against the pads of my fingertips. I can't help but explore his torso, tracing the lines of his chest and trailing back down to his stomach.

Nothing can ever be the same between us. I melt into him, pressing my chest against his, and I feel his heart racing as quickly as mine.

Jack Nelson owns me, every piece.

"You okay?"

I close my eyes and wish I could go back to that day when everything was simpler. "Yeah."

Evan scoots closer until our shoulders are touching. "Tell me what happened. Talk to me, Evie. Get it out. You'll feel better."

I've never told anyone about this place or what it means to me. Even sharing it with Evan isn't easy. "It's where we had our first kiss and he asked me to be his girlfriend."

"Ah."

I place my head against Evan's shoulder and sigh. "I thought he was my forever." How I had hoped he would be, but everything changed once I left for Germany.

Evan's protective arm wraps around my shoulder before he kisses the top of my head. "He still can be."

I wish I could believe that's true. Especially after seeing him again and realizing the feelings never faded. "Let's not talk about fairy tales anymore. They aren't real. They don't happen in real life."

At least, not in mine.

"It's not a fairy tale. Based on the way he stalked toward you and then rescued you, I'd say he's still in love with you, Evie. That fine specimen of man is crazy about you."

"It's just Jack. He's always been overprotective," I argue.

"Uh-huh," he mutters and pulls me backward as he lies back on the grass. "Look at that cloud." He points toward an oblong cloud straight above us.

"What about it?" I settle into the crook of his arm and gaze at the fluffy clouds against the bright blue sky, feeling more content.

"It looks like a penis."

I start to giggle and shake my head. "You think everything looks like a penis."

"Or a cupcake," he corrects me. "There's no two things more delicious."

"I'd have to agree." I turn on my side, curling against him. "Don't you wish you could find someone to settle down with?"

"I have you, darlin'. What more can a guy ask for?"

"Penis," I say through my laughter.

"You are missing the vital parts, for sure. But as long as I have you by my side, I'm a happy man."

"Evan, be serious. You need to find a man to love."

"So do you."

"Maybe a certain doctor is waiting for you to call. He was into you."

"We were talking about you, Evie. Not me."

I roll my eyes and give up, lying back down to stare up at the penis cloud with him.

He and I are broken. We've been this way since the day we met. It's what makes us a perfect twosome. There's only so much ugly a person can take in their life before snapping, and Evan and I hit that limit and came out on the other side—but not unscathed.

"Let's make a deal, Evie."

"Sure."

I'm skeptical. He comes up with some harebrained ideas and usually finds a way to rope me in because I'm a complete sucker. He knows I am a pushover at times. He tells me I am too nice for my own good.

"When you find love and finally allow it into your life, I'll find my forever too."

"If it were only that easy."

"But I won't leave your side until then," he assures me.

"It's a deal," I tell him, but I know it's not fair.

He shouldn't keep himself attached to me. I don't know if I'll ever be able to move on from my love for Jack. The past is the past, and the future seems too bleak to think that anything good could happen. Maybe I'll get lucky and Evan will find someone to love before I drag him into old age with me. Because at the rate we are going, that is exactly where we are headed…old and alone.

JACK

Jason sits down and pulls one of the beers I ordered in front of him. “Thanks for inviting me. I don’t have many friends around here anymore.”

“I don’t understand what happened because you were always popular, man.” Everyone loved him when we were in school. He was one of the most well-liked guys in our grade. Hell, I had always thought if Evie weren’t with me, she would date him or someone like him. If she had turned me down when I asked her to be mine, it might have changed everything, but she was meant to be mine.

His shoulders fall forward as he twists the beer in his hands. “Drugs happened.” The bottle slides across the table, making small water rings on the wood. “I became the biggest dick. I’m still trying to earn back the trust of a lot of people, starting with my family.”

“How the hell did you get so lost?”

His fingers pick at the edges of the label of the beer

bottle as he gathers his thoughts. “Los Angeles isn’t for the faint of heart. I had big-city dreams when I moved there. The parties weren’t like here, and I didn’t know how to control myself. Any drug you want, it’s already there, waiting for you to try it. Fuck.” He scrubs his hand down his face. “I wasn’t thinking. I thought I could control myself. I thought I could handle it. But in the end, it took over my life. The choices I made ruined me.”

“I never got into that shit. Drugs just never appealed to me.” I never would have thought Jason would get into that whole scene. He was always so level-headed.

“I wanted to fit in, Jack. Everyone else was doing it, so I figured, why not? Stupid mistake.” He shakes his head and stares down at his beer.

“What happened, man?”

“I flunked out and came back home. It took about a month before my mom figured it out. She put an end to it real quick.”

“She did the right thing, man. I’m glad she was able to get you help.”

“Yeah, I know it now, but I didn’t then. I was so angry with her for making me go to rehab. In my mind, everyone else was in the wrong. I didn’t think I had a problem.”

“Addicts usually don’t.”

“I screwed everything up. I could’ve had an amazing life. Sure, I am doing okay now, but it hasn’t been easy to get to this point.”

“But think of the difference you’re making.” I’m trying to be positive. The poor guy doesn’t look like he can take much more.

“Yeah.” He smiles, finally looking me in the eye again.

"I do, but it's still here." His eyes drift around the room, and he shrugs. "In the Hollow."

"It's not such a bad place," I tell him because it still feels like home. No matter how much I wanted to escape as a kid, I feel comfortable here. There's a familiarity that I can't find anywhere else in the world—even Philadelphia.

"Yeah. Well. I saw Renee today," he says through clenched teeth.

My fist balls up, and every muscle in my body tenses at the mention of her name. "I hate that bitch."

"I know. Me too."

"I don't know who's worse, her or Jess."

He leans back, crossing his arms in front of his chest. "It's debatable."

"She was at the store today. They both were. Invited me over." I snort.

"Did she come on to you?" He raises an eyebrow.

I roll my eyes. "Yes. Guess I'm not *that* special."

"Nope." He tips his chair back like he used to do in high school, teetering on two legs and about to fall over. "She's trash, and he pretends not to see it."

"They're fucked up. Pathetic, really."

"You have no idea."

"But." I lean forward and rub the back of my neck. "They said something about Evie that kind of has me questioning everything."

He starts to fall backward and grabs on to the table before he topples back. "Shit. Don't believe anything those two say." His eyes dart to the right. "Don't look now, but she just walked in."

"Evie?" I want to turn around, but I don't want to seem

overeager. Who the hell am I fooling? I'm always eager when it comes to Evie. After six years, I'll take every chance I can get to be near her. "She's here?"

He nods. "Yep. She's lookin' fine too." He whistles quietly so only I can hear. "She just sat down at the bar."

I turn the chair so I'm facing her direction. Evie hops off the barstool, and for a second, I think she's going to come my way, but she starts poking that Evan guy in the chest.

I wish I could read her lips, but her back's to me and Evan's laughing. He grabs her around the waist and hauls her between his legs.

She's mine.

My insides twist, and my fists tighten at my sides. He hugs her securely, with his hands roaming down her back, and I force myself to stay seated. Although what I really want is to run to her, throw her over my shoulder, and haul ass out of here.

"Looks pretty cozy over there," Jason says, twisting the knife that's already lodged in my chest.

I know what he's doing. He's trying to get me to go over there, but Evie hasn't bothered to reach out to me. She knows I'm here, yet nothing. She's ignoring my presence.

"I need another drink," I mutter, keeping my gaze locked on her.

"Another round of Jack," he tells the waitress even though we haven't touched the shots I ordered before he arrived.

"Coming right up," she says.

"Go over there," Jason encourages me.

"Not yet."

When the waitress sets the drinks down, I pull one in front of me before she even has a chance to walk away. "Anything else?"

"We're good." I wave her off.

Jason thrusts his shot glass in front of me after I swallow mine down. "Should we drink to something?" he asks, holding his beer as I grab the shot glass.

"I just need to drink." I keep my eyes on Evie and Evan.

"I haven't done a shot in years."

"I'll drink for the both of us. You can drive me home."

He rolls his eyes. "Sounds like a fun night."

I tip my head back, letting the liquid slide down my throat.

"You may want to pace yourself," Jason says. "You won't find the answers you seek at the bottom of that glass. Trust me, I tried. It doesn't work."

"I don't need a counselor," I tell him, feeling the liquor taking hold and lightening the burden of regret that's been sitting on my shoulders.

Right now, the only thing I want is my lips against hers. I need to make her mine again, and I'm going to make it happen.

She gets up and walks toward the bathroom, and I know it may be my only chance to talk with her without Evan keeping a watchful eye.

I follow, entranced by the way her hips swing as she enters the hallway. Even in the semidarkness with only dim lighting overhead, I can still see the perfect sway.

I'm tucked into the back corner, out of the way but

within arm's reach of the door. A few people wander out, and each time the door opens, my heart leaps and then is crushed when I see it isn't her. If I wouldn't get thrown out of the place, I'd kick everyone out of the bathroom and lock us inside.

Leaning against the wall, I wait as patiently as I can. The alcohol in my system is cheering me on and making my judgment a little fuzzy because in no way is this a good idea.

When the door finally opens and Evie steps out, I grab her by the arm and haul her backward, spinning her around to face me. Her eyes are wide as she collides with my chest.

"Evie," I whisper and drink her in.

Her hand pushes against my front as she tries to wiggle free of my hold, but I don't give her the chance to get away before my lips crash down on hers.

At first, she doesn't kiss me back, but she's no longer struggling to get away. I wrap my arm around her middle and pull her closer, leaving no space between us.

Then it happens.

Her desire takes over as she melts into me and brings her arms around my neck.

The kiss isn't like any we've had before.

We were kids the last time we were in this position, and the kiss wasn't as hungry.

Time has done this.

Distance and time have made the need for each other grow.

I figured she was lost forever, but now that she's in

front of me, attached to me at the mouth, I'm not letting her go again.

Our tongues tangle together, needy in their dance around each other. Her breathing is ragged just like mine as the kiss grows more demanding.

Trying to get closer, I slide my hand up her back and tangle it in the back of her silky hair, holding her to me. I place my other hand at the small of her back so that every inch of my body that can touch her is.

God, she feels remarkable in my arms.

Her tiny moans vibrate through my body, causing my cock to grow. It makes the need to be inside her so strong that, in my alcohol-induced haze, I know I'd fuck her right here, right now.

We gasp for air and stare into each other's eyes without saying a word. There's nothing that needs to be said. No denial can be believable after a kiss like that.

We both want each other.

The feelings we had years ago still simmer under the surface.

It doesn't matter if she's with Evan; she still wants me.

"Evie." My hand slides down her back, resting on her ass as I give it a firm squeeze, pressing her middle into my erection. "I want you," I tell her as our gazes are locked and hungry. "I need to be inside you." I thrust my cock against her ever so slightly, and her eyes roll back in her head. "You want it too."

"I can't," she whispers back but doesn't pull away.

"You can." There's nothing she can say to make me believe that she feels that way.

Evie sucks in a breath and exhales slowly. Her hands

slide down my front and come to a rest on my chest. "Jack, let me go." She starts to push away, and I grip her tighter. "I can't do this. We can't do this," she pleads.

"We did. You kissed me back. You love the way my arms feel wrapped around you. The way my touch makes you feel alive. I feel that for you too, Evie."

"Is there a problem here?" a woman asks after walking out of the bathroom and being nosy like most people in Ridge Hollow.

"No problem," I tell her without looking up.

"I have to go," Evie says, pushing against my chest harder and ignoring the woman standing behind us.

I tilt my head down, my breath tickling her neck. My lips are caressing her earlobe as I speak. "Just remember, you'll always belong to me, Evie. Always," I tell her, finally releasing my hold on her.

She stands there for a minute and gapes at me without saying a word. Her lips are so bee-stung from our kiss that she'll be unable to hide it from Evan.

I want him to know she's mine. She always has been, and soon she'll be in my arms permanently.

"That won't happen again. I'm not yours anymore." Her fingers glide over her swollen lips. The memory of the kiss has to be playing through her mind. I know it is in mine.

Damn, her lips tasted good.

"Lie to yourself all you want. You still love me."

She glares at me and lets out a soft grunt before turning her back on me, marching toward Evan.

She can run back to him and play it safe for now, but it

won't last. I'm under her skin as much as she's under mine.

Jason's waiting for me when I return, tipped back in his chair with a big ole shit-eating grin on his face. "Whatever you did really pissed her off. She flew out of here as soon as she came out." Jason laughs.

"She's just mad that she still loves me." I grin. I'm tempted to push it away and go after her, but I stay to let her have time to come to her senses.

Buzzed or not, I know I love Evie and that she'll always be mine.

EVIE

I can't sleep.

Every time I close my eyes, the memory of kissing Jack keeps playing through my mind. I give up and grab my robe off the end of the bed and tighten the tie at my waist. I tiptoe down the hallway to the stairs in an effort not to wake Evan.

When I round the corner to the kitchen, he's sitting at the island counter. "Can't sleep?" he asks, tracing the rim of a mug with his index finger.

"No." I turn on the teakettle to make myself a cup of tea before leaning on the counter across from him.

"Why don't you just give in to him already? You know you love him, and he loves you."

I cover my face with my hands. "You don't understand. I'm not that girl anymore. Things have changed."

"Whatever happened in the past is the past. I can tell you still love him. Don't try to deny it either. You aren't fooling me or yourself. You know it. There's no one else you talk about and light up the way you do when you mention his name."

I groan, letting my arms flatten against the Formica counter, and I rest my forehead against my forearms. "He threw me away, Evan. When I needed him the most, he threw me away like I meant nothing."

He broke his promise to me. Jack promised me forever, and after a few months, he was done waiting.

"You were kids, Evie."

I lift my head, just enough to stare him straight in the eyes. "We weren't ten. He said he loved me. He said he'd always be there for me. When I needed him the most, he vanished. He let me down, Evan. I can't forget the past. I wish I could."

The whistle of the teakettle deters Evan from saying whatever intelligent, witty thing he was about to spout. I right myself and turn my back, plucking a bag of Earl Grey from the tin.

Evan's studying me, watching me closely as I slide my mug of hot water across the counter and walk toward him before taking a seat on the stool next to him.

I can feel the judgment in his eyes, but I don't dare look at him. No one knows me better. Jack did once, but now it's Evan and me against the world. He knows all my secrets, every fear I've ever had and every nightmare I've lived through in my short twenty-three years.

He knows I'm lying and avoiding how I really feel. I've never loved another person the way I loved Jack. I never gave anyone a chance to get that close to me. Just

Evan, but then, he's gay, and there was never a chance we could become anything more than friends. There was no danger to my heart with him. Jack holds the power to destroy me. I don't think I could survive it if he hurt me again.

"I won't let you ruin this," he says softly.

Looping my finger around the tiny string, I dip my tea bag inside the mug repeatedly. "There's nothing to ruin."

He shakes his head and gives me a judgmental sideways glance. "I think I have a hard head. But, man, you sure know how to hold your ground."

We sit in the relative darkness of the kitchen, just the light above the stove creating a warm glow in the tiny space. I ponder his statement for a minute as my tea turns just the right shade, and I pull the bag out, setting it on a dish in front of us.

Am I being stubborn? I don't think so. Jack still hasn't acknowledged what he did.

Has so much time passed that I should just forgive and forget?

Too much has happened for it to be that simple. There's more than just the fact that he forgot me and threw me away. Things have happened that Jack may never forgive me for if he finds out. I've spent six years with the memory of our relationship haunting me, while he moved on.

He forgot about me so easily, as if I had never mattered. As if what we shared wasn't special or maybe even real. No, that's a lie. I know it was real. The connection we shared is still there. I can't deny that, but…

"He didn't want me before he saw me, Evan. I was just a memory to him. Once we're gone, he'll forget me again."

"I've seen the way he looks at you. He might have forgotten you before, but now…he's not going to be able to. That man wants you and, girl, he intends on having you."

"There's no going back," I tell him before blowing across the surface of my tea in hopes I don't burn the shit out of my mouth as I take my first sip.

Evan gently squeezes my free hand, being my rock like always. "Why don't you just tell him, then? Why are you so worried he'll be mad? If you don't want him back, tell him, and let him be so angry he never wants you again."

"I can't do that."

My stomach turns at the thought of telling Jack about the one thing I've kept hidden from everyone in my life except for Evan.

At times, I lie to myself and pretend it never happened. It's easier that way. My heart aches a little less with the fairy tale I choose to believe instead of the cold, hard reality of a secret I've kept hidden.

Evan turns toward me, setting his cup down. He props his elbow on the counter and rests his head in the palm of his hand. "This is why I'm gay. I'll never understand women."

I laugh softly and turn to face him. "You're gay because you like dick. No man understands women, so you can't use that as an excuse."

He laughs. "That's true. Very true. Cock is the best, isn't it? And you're right, women are so messed up." His eyes are bulging out as he shakes his head.

Evan and I met during senior year. We had been dragged around the world by our parents. Neither of us was happy about it either. We became friends, both miserable in Germany and ready to break free as soon as we received our diplomas and earned our freedom from military life.

We spent a few years backpacking around Europe, trying to forget our pasts and make a new future. I didn't have time to fall in love, nor did I want to.

I had Evan.

What more could a girl want?

He's my companion, the best friend I have ever had. We clung to each other and formed a new family. When he came out to his parents right after graduation, they shunned him. Especially his father. The angry, hateful names he called Evan can never be forgotten or forgiven.

My relationship with my parents quickly deteriorated too. When I told them I was putting off college for a few years to travel, they were dismayed.

My father ordered me to enroll in college or join the service, but I just laughed. By the time I said goodbye, there was so much hostility, they were happy to see me go. Our relationship had never been an easy one. It stung a little, but I had been planning my escape from them even when I was back here and dreaming of a future with Jack.

Evan and I became a team and our own little family. We've been like this for five years. Nothing and no one has come between us. They never will.

Letting Jack in again feels wrong. Even if I did love him, I would feel I was giving up the last person I could depend on for someone who had crushed me in my past.

As if he can read my mind, Evan says, “You’ll always be my family, Evie.”

I drag my gaze to his and smile softly as tears start to form in my eyes. “You’re all I have left, Evan.”

He tucks a lock of hair behind my ear. “That’s not true. You have other people who love you just as much.”

I know he’s talking about Jack. Everyone else is gone. My mother died two years after I left Germany, and my father had a massive heart attack a month ago. His remains are sitting in an urn in my bedroom, waiting to be buried in the family plot at Ridge Hollow cemetery.

“I’m scared.”

“Take a chance. Sometimes, you just gotta leap, darling.”

“When are you going to leap, sweetheart?” I try to take the pressure off me and put it on him.

We’re quite the messed-up pair.

Evan hasn’t tried to find love. He’s always with me. We both stay in our little bubble, unwilling to let ourselves get hurt. He is just as afraid as I am. We use each other to protect our hearts. No one can hurt us if we don’t let them in. But Jack has been in my heart since the day we met. He will always have the biggest pieces of it too.

“As soon as I know you’re okay.”

“I’m fine,” I scoff, tipping my chin to call bullshit on his statement. “You’re just making an excuse.”

“I’m doing no such thing. We made a pact years ago. I never forgot it.”

“We were kids, Evan. You can’t live by something we promised each other when we were nineteen.”

“But you punish Jack for something that happened

before that. Why shouldn't I be held to the same standard?"

I walked right into that one.

"Nice." I twist the mug in my hand, staring down into the contents like it's going to show me what I should do, but nothing happens.

"The truth stinks sometimes." He slaps me in the face with my own words, giving me nowhere to hide from a truth I can no longer deny. Evan turns back toward his tea, and we sit in comfortable silence.

Opening myself up to Jack won't be so easy a second time. With so much distance shared between us, there may be no going back to where we left off. Too much has happened, at least, in my life. I'm not sure where his life has taken him, but somehow, we're both in Ridge Hollow at the same time.

I've been back before, usually staying under the radar and never running into him. I've slipped in and out without being noticed by too many. But I've never stayed this long.

It's Evan's fault we made this trip longer. Every time we came, he fell in love with the quaintness of the small town. He mumbled some mumbo jumbo about how it reminded him of many of the small villages we visited in Europe and how he felt at home here.

I let him talk me into renting a house for a month, although I told him we wouldn't stay longer than two weeks. He laughed as he always did and told me to let things unfold on their own. He wanted time to explore what Ridge Hollow had to offer even though I told him it was just a tiny country town in the middle of nowhere.

I couldn't deny feeling as if I finally had come home

again. Even though I only spent four years of my life here, nowhere else felt this right. I had so many great memories that surrounded me at every turn that I couldn't deny it was truly the one place that felt like home.

I can't help but wonder if it's fate that has brought me here. I don't know how else to explain it. Could I give Jack a second chance? My mind screams no, but my heart cries yes.

"I'm going to pick up the dry cleaning for the funeral tomorrow," Evan says as I sip my coffee in the breakfast nook of our rental home the next morning, barely able to form words after my sleepless night.

The morning sunshine lights up the entire space, giving it a heavenly glow. It's become my favorite spot in the house.

"Do you want me to come?" I ask even though I'm still in my robe and in no mood to face the world.

"Nah, you stay here and relax." He kisses me on the top of the head before he grabs his keys off the counter. "Call me if you need anything," he says as he walks toward the front door and I follow him.

Ever since I laid eyes on Jack, he's all I can think about. Him and the secret I've kept from him for so long it weighs me down like a thick, wet blanket. I should've told him long ago; every year that passes makes the secret more cumbersome and causes the guilt to seep deeper into my bones. I need to tell him and pray that he forgives me for waiting so long to tell him the truth.

We can't move forward until I go back, uncovering the one thing I've tried to forget.

It's time to face the past and tell Jack the truth.

JACK

Waking up in a cold sweat, I kick off the covers and stare at the ceiling. My vision blurs as I try to focus on the tiny cracks that creep out from the edges of my Elle McPherson poster on the ceiling from my senior year.

My head's pounding, and the small amount of light in the room isn't helping the hangover that's going to knock me on my ass for half of the day.

I shouldn't have had so much to drink, but at the time, it seemed like a good idea.

I dreamed of Evie.

The way she smelled of strawberry from her lip gloss.

The feel of her lips against mine as we kissed.

The sound of her moans.

Every moment of my sleep was filled with thoughts of her, taunting me.

Blinking a few times, I remember the last words she

ever sent to me just months after she left, feeling the sting as if it was only yesterday.

Jack,

I said I'd come back for you, but I can't keep that promise. Please move on without me. Although I loved you from the moment I saw you, some things aren't meant to be. Don't contact me. I've changed my number. This is the only way I can break free from you. Let me go, Jack, and I will do the same for you.

Evie

I'd read it at least a hundred times before the paper finally disintegrated into tiny little shreds. I couldn't believe it. We had plans. She promised she loved me forever and ever.

I kept writing her, but every letter was returned unopened. I finally threw in the towel and gave up on our forever somewhere around Christmas. What could I do if she refused to contact me? I had no way of trying to talk to her.

Moving on without her was the hardest thing I ever did, but I played it off around my friends. Everyone in the Hollow figured I ended things with Evie because she was half a world away. Only Jason knew exactly how crushed I was when she gave up on us.

Once word spread during Christmas break that I was back on the market, my phone didn't stop ringing. The line of "Hollow Hotties," as Jason called them, vying for my attention was staggering, but they kept me busy until graduation.

But none of them made me forget about Evie, no matter how hard I tried. She was always in the back of my mind. Evie was the only girl I wanted, and I couldn't have her.

Rolling to my side, I glance at the tall glass of water and two aspirin lying on my nightstand. I guess I didn't sneak into the house as quietly as I thought last night. I swallow the pills and check the time on my phone. I send Jason a text asking him if he knows where Evie is staying, and he replies quickly with an address not far from my mom's.

Even though my head feels like it's ready to explode, I shower, dress, and grab a cup of coffee before heading to her address.

I've waited six years to talk to her, and I am not about to waste another moment. We have things to discuss. I'm owed an explanation for the way she threw me to the side and for her admission that she hated me.

"You're hitting creeper status," I say to myself as I switch off the engine, parking just down the street from Evie's.

I know this isn't how to do it, but I can't figure out another way to find out what happened. Just as I'm about to settle in, the door opens, and Evie and Evan walk out onto the front porch. She rests her body against the railing with her arms crossed in front of her, and Evan stands two feet away, animated as he speaks with his arms flailing about.

She starts to laugh, sliding her hands down to her stomach. Evan laughs too and takes a bow before trotting down the front steps and hopping on his aqua scooter.

Guys in this town have trucks and bigger trucks, but seeing him on a scooter reminds me of the people back in

Philly, not in Ridge Hollow. Not even the older people around here have scooters. The terrain and country roads aren't the best, and a scooter is just…well, silly.

Evie waves to him with a smile as he backs down the driveway, giving her a double honk. It sounds more like a squeak in its ridiculousness before he drives away in the opposite direction, keeping my cover intact.

Her smile fades as soon as he's out of sight. She drops onto the porch swing, wrapping her robe tightly around her body, and closes her eyes, basking in the sunlight.

She's always been so full of life, but something has changed. I can see it. Not just when she looks at me, but it's written all over her face. She's scarred. Different from how she was in our youth. The sadness is deeper than when she kissed me goodbye.

I'm out of the truck before I have time to think about what I'm doing or how she'll react. I'm drawn to her, to her unhappiness, and to the hazy memory of our kiss last night.

My body craves her, wanting to console her like I did when she was mine. I want to take away her sadness and bring her back to the girl I knew, the happy one who had the world stretched out before her, a million possibilities within reach.

Her head slowly turns in my direction as I walk up the driveway. She stands, her gorgeous blue eyes growing wider with each determined step I take toward her.

She comes to the edge of the porch, and for a moment, I think she's excited to see me. "Jack." She grips the railing and sways back on her heels. "What are you doing here?"

"Where did your boyfriend go?"

"He's not my boyfriend, but he'd like to be yours." She smiles softly, trying to defuse the situation because the tension in the air is palpable.

Her statement almost knocks me backward. Like a fool, I've been stewing about another man touching her since I first saw her. "He's gay?" I have to repeat the words because they don't seem real or even remotely true.

"Sadly, he is."

"You lied to me, Evie."

"I know. I'm sorry. It just felt right," she says, like it's no big deal.

My foot touches the top step, and I want to grab her in my arms and kiss her again, but I don't. "Six fuckin' years without a word."

She swallows hard, her eyes dipping toward the porch floor, avoiding my eyes. "Yeah."

The feelings I felt when she wrote me that letter all those years ago have clawed their way to the surface. I narrow my gaze, suddenly filled with anger and fear. "Did you ever love me?"

"Of course," she whispers, and her head jerks backward.

Taking a step forward, I close the gap between us. "Evie." I reach out, gently wrapping my hand behind her neck and bringing her eyes to mine so the message isn't lost. "I never stopped loving you."

Her blue eyes pierce my soul, filled with warmth and longing, but also something else I can't quite place. "I loved you more than the moon and stars, Jack. How could you ever think I didn't?"

"You haven't forgotten, have you? You said you'd love me forever, and then…"

"I did," she whispers as I bring our lips close enough to touch, and her eyes dip to my mouth.

"But you didn't."

"I do, Jack. I do," she says with conviction.

My lips cover hers, and my fingers tighten around the back of her neck. There's still a hint of the strawberry lip gloss I've never forgotten as my tongue sweeps across the familiar ridges of her bottom lip, the ones that teased me in my youth.

Placing her hand against my chest, she returns the kiss. It's not the kiss of a friend, but of a long-lost lover who's missed my touch as much as I've missed hers. It's different from last night. There's no fight in her when she touches me.

Just as my heart is about to do a flip, filled with so much excitement that she's finally going to admit she wants me, she pushes herself back, breaking our connection. "Wait, Jack. Stop."

Nipping her lip with my teeth, I groan and want to lose myself in her again. "Don't make me stop. Not now. I can't." I moan softly, unable to hold it back.

"I won't."

Holding her neck with one hand, I loop my arm around her waist and pull her body against me. When she doesn't say anything, I cover her mouth again, silencing her before she can protest.

The sweet part in her lips widens, inviting me in fully as her hands tangle in my hair and curl around the ends with her fingertips. I hold her so close there is no space left between us.

Her heartbeat is as erratic as her breathing. Her chest moves against mine, pressing her breasts into me. Tempting me to claim her heart and her body as I did years ago.

It's my turn to push back, my breathing ragged and uneven as I rest my forehead against hers. "I want you so fucking bad, Evie." I close my eyes and breathe her in. "For six years, I've waited for the day I could touch you again."

"Don't stop," she moans into my mouth, sweeping her tongue along mine in a lover's caress.

I don't plan on ever stopping.

Now that I know she really does still love me, I will never let her go.

"I see you two are up to your old tricks again," Mrs. Griffin, notorious town busybody, says from behind us.

Evie peers over my shoulder and sighs. "Hi, Mrs. Griffin. It's always a pleasure to see you."

"Don't lie to her. She's an asshole," I growl. Damn her for interrupting when things were finally getting started.

"You two better take that inside. Wouldn't want any torrid rumors to start."

"Come inside," Evie says, taking a step backward and pulling me with her.

This business of Evie not being with me ends today.

EVIE

"I've missed you, Evie."

Every muscle in my body seizes with the memory of the way Jack made me feel. God, the man used to play me like a fine instrument even though we were barely adults. He knew all the right ways to touch me to drive me wild. If I let him, he'd get me off track and headed down the very path I should avoid.

"Jack, I have to tell you something first. It's important."

He comes up behind me and places his mouth against my ear, resting his firm hands just under my breasts. The contact sends shivers through my body and causes my breathing to falter. "Remember how good we were together?" His thumb brushes over my nipple, and it hardens from the sensation.

I inhale and close my eyes. "I do."

How could I forget?

I squeeze my eyes shut, trying to chase away the flashbacks that are taunting me. A steady ache settles between my legs when he presses his erection against my back, and my resistance slips.

"Imagine how it would be now that we know what we're doing," he taunts, tempting me to beg him to take me right now, right here. Whoever is watching, be damned.

He turns me around, gazing down at me with such love and desire that I'm ready to give in if I'm not careful.

His lips brush over the freckles that dust the corner of my eye, nearly forcing me to my knees. His touch is driving me so close to the brink of insanity fueled by lust.

"We have a lot to talk about. We've been apart too long to just fall right back into old habits."

God, I still love this man.

Why does this have to be so complicated?

There's nothing I'd love more than to fall back into us. Picking up right where we left off as if nothing has happened to either of us since we were together six years ago. But too much has occurred. Too many bad things have come to pass for us to just let our bodies and even our hearts permit all reason to be thrown out the window.

"Is that all I was to you?" His brows furrow, and I can see anger in his eyes. "A habit?"

I shake my head. "No," I whisper, moving my lips near his, and I regret hurting him any more than necessary, but I must do it. It's just as much for his protection as it is mine. "You were my everything, Jack, and then you were nothing." I shake his hold and take a few steps back.

He reaches for me, and I have nowhere to go as he wraps his arms around my body and captures me in a warm embrace. "I won't let you pull away from me. Not now."

"I'm not."

But I am. I need to pull away.

This is going to crush us both all over again.

For the sake of my heart, I need to run or, at the very least, put a little space between us until I tell him everything that's happened. That will cool him off enough that I'll no longer have to fight off his advances. Jack Nelson will leave me in the dust and never come back again. I will never survive it, but Evan will be here to catch me when I fall.

Jack's lips find the spot that makes me weak in the knees. "I haven't even been here five minutes, and I feel you withdrawing."

"I'm nervous," I say and mutter a few more words, but I'm so lost in the feel of his lips against my skin that I'm not even sure what I said.

He's kissing me, driving me wild and working me up like he used to. He feels so good. His hardness against me. It's been so long since I've had anyone touch me that I crave his warmth and embrace. My willpower is slipping, and there's nothing I can do to stop it. He's too close, and I'm consumed with him. I see the freight train coming, but I can't step out of the way.

"Give in to me, Evie. Be mine again."

"Jack."

God, I want to say yes.

I want to feel him deep inside me and relish in the weight of his body against mine. There's nothing more I want in the world than to get lost in him.

"I still love you," he whispers in my ear before retracing the line of my neck with his lips. Slowly, brick by brick, the wall of resistance I had built up begins to crumble.

When he slides his palm up my side and holds my breast in his hand, my body quakes with excitement. I lose my breath when his thumb grazes my nipple again, and the need I feel for him becomes overpowering. Warmth pools in my lower belly and travels down to the core of my desire.

"There's my girl."

"I need to tell you something." My statement is met by another sweep of his finger against my hardened nipple.

"Will it ruin this?" His cock pokes me in the back, and my body tightens.

I shiver with need and tip my head back as another brick falls to the ground. "Probably," I say through my lusty haze.

"Don't tell me," he whispers, his tongue brushing over my ear. "I don't want to stop." A whimper escapes me as he presses against me, reminding me of what I have been missing.

"But it's important."

"I want to make love to you, Evie. Whatever you've got to say can wait. It's waited this long. What's another few hours?" he murmurs, running his fingers along my ribs.

My stomach flips at the thought of him touching me over and over again. "Few hours?"

"I need to savor you and take my time. I have years to

make up for." He cradles my face in his hand, and I'm a goner.

"We should really talk," I say one final time. I'm almost panting. I know it. He knows it too. He has me right where he wants me, and there's nothing I can do or say except blurt out the words I've held inside for so long.

He doesn't give me a chance to say the one thing that's been hanging between us. He smashes the final brick when his lips seal over mine, and he takes my breath away with the most passionate kiss, plundering my mouth like he's exploring new territory and claiming my body as his bounty. I'm helpless to fight him off because I want this. I need this as desperately as he does.

Jack lifts me off the floor and cradles me in his arms. Our lips are sealed, and everything else around us falls away as he quickly jogs up the stairs as if I weigh nothing.

"Last door on the left," I say into his mouth, unable to break contact even for a second.

We don't make it to my bed. He kicks the bedroom door shut before letting my body slide down his, pressing me up against the back of the door. The robe gives little resistance to his quick fingers.

His fingers ravage me, pushing aside the crotch of my panties and thrusting inside of me as we kiss. I'm helpless to stop him. I ride his hand like a horny kid, relishing the contact and warmth of his body against mine. It's been so long since I've come at the hands of someone else, and let's be honest…this is Jack. I can't stop him. I dig my fingernails into his skin and let him take me.

His thumb presses on my sensitive bundle of nerves as

his fingers bring me such pleasure. Harder and faster, his digits work me over.

Within minutes, I'm close. The edge is so near that I can't stop. Jack pulls his lips from mine and stares down at me as he increases the pace, watching his fingers as they scissor in and out of my tight warmth. I ride his hand faster, the intensity of his gaze overwhelming my senses.

When my insides start to twist and my toes curl against the carpet, Jack's strong arm keeps me upright as the waves of pleasure shoot from my core through every fiber of my being.

"Oh, Jack." I'm gasping, trying to regain my senses after one of the most devastating orgasms I've had in my life. It's no use when Jack grabs me by the ass, and my legs wrap around his waist as if I've done it every day of my life. He carries me toward the bed, and I'm powerless to stop him because I'm so sated that my muscles feel heavy and useless.

When he lays me down and backs away, all I can do is stare at him. Everything about his body has changed since the last time I saw him naked. My mouth waters, and my pussy springs back to life when his washboard abs and thick muscles come into view as he pulls his T-shirt over his head. *Sweet Jesus.* My fingers itch to touch him, but I gawk instead like I've never seen him naked before.

He's beautiful. A true work of art. Gone is the boy's body I once worshiped, replaced by the beast of a man he has become.

I ache for him. It's the same ache that I had the first time he made love to me. I knew then, as I know now, that I am a goner.

There's no recovering.

No getting over him a second time.

I finally come to terms with the one thing I've been lying to myself about for years.

I've always belonged to Jack Nelson.

"Make love to me, Jack."

Jack crawls onto the bed, covering my body with his. When our bodies collide, I know I will never be the same.

Taking his time, Jack ravishes my body with his mouth. Starting at my neck, he traces a path along my pulse to my collarbone, nipping my skin at just the right spot. I shiver under his weight and wrap my legs around his waist, pulling his body closer.

His body is bigger than the last time we were in this same position. Both of ours are. We're no longer kids, unsure and careful in our touches. We're hungry, almost to the point of famine, with an insatiable appetite for each other. Our hands move quickly across the other's skin, feeling every dip and curve as his mouth continues its descent over my torso.

I lie back, closing my eyes and basking in the feel of him against me. His palm closes around my breast, and I ache to feel his tongue against me. "Jack," I moan.

As if he can read my mind, his lips close around the tip, and I melt into the bed. I'm drunk on lust. Lost in love with Jack. It's been six years since anyone has touched me.

I dig my fingers into his hair and hold his face against my breast. My toes curl, and my breath hitches as his tongue sweeps across the top, sending shock waves through my system. He grinds his hips against me, driving me wild and quickly close to the edge of orgasm.

God, I've missed this. Missed the feel of him against me. Missed the sounds he makes deep in his throat as he kisses my body.

I slide my hands down his back before reaching between us and fumbling with his belt.

He scoots down my body, breaking my hold on his pants. "Not yet," he growls, licking my skin at the edge of my panties. "I want to taste you."

My insides rejoice at his words. I want him to taste me too. I want him to taste every inch of my body. He stares down at me, looking over my body with such reverence that any nervousness I have drifts away.

"I love you," I say with a soft smile. I do. I love the man before me, grown-up and fierce.

"I love you too, Evie girl." He settles between my legs, never taking his eyes off mine as his lips close around my most sensitive spot.

For a few moments, I'm unable to form any thoughts. His mouth is just that good. The world around us seems to evaporate as if we're the only two people left on the planet.

Every caress of his tongue sears my skin with such passion. He's marking my body, claiming me once and for all as his. Not that I have ever belonged to anyone else.

Jack Nelson is all I have ever known.

He is all I have ever craved.

I lose track of time and the number of orgasms he's able to pull out of me before I'm left gasping for air. My body shakes under his touch as he inches his way up my body and kicks off his pants.

“Say you want me,” he says as his cock hovers at my opening.

“I want you.”

His fingers laced with mine, Jack pins my hands over my head before capturing my lips with his. He gently pushes the head of his cock inside before seating himself fully. I moan softly, loving the fullness of him inside me.

Our bodies rock together in perfect harmony, never missing a beat. Jack’s eyes never waver from mine as he takes his time making love to me.

He loves me.

I love him.

That’s never changed, not with distance or time. Love isn’t something that can be swept away or forgotten so easily or so quickly. Six years may seem like an eternity, but when there’s true love, the kind that has been permanently etched on your soul… it’s no time at all.

JACK

It's dark outside when I finally open my eyes. I've been in bed with Evie for hours, snuggling, fucking, and touching. Exploring each other's bodies as if it were the first time.

Her hand is tucked under the pillow, and her blond hair is cascading over the sheets like a waterfall of gold as she breathes deeply through her parted, full lips.

I could lie here for an eternity and be content. She doesn't even need to speak to me. Merely having her by my side is enough. This is better than anything I've done in the last six years. For the first time in a long time, I feel whole. I feel at peace, but that doesn't stop the memories.

"My father is going to kill me," Evie says, scrambling around the barn and picking up her clothes that were discarded around our blanket.

I prop myself up on my elbow and watch her as she panics. "The damage is done, love. Just lie back down with me."

She shakes her head and is on the verge of tears as she pulls her white cotton panties up her legs. "He's going to ground me for all eternity."

She's being a little dramatic, but not by much. Her father is probably going to ground her for at least a month for not calling or being home by curfew. "Then lie with me for a little while longer. It's going to be a while before we can do it again."

She yanks her T-shirt over her head and then stands there, staring down at me as she thinks over what I just said. "I don't know, Jack. I'm already two hours late."

"Just give me another ten minutes. I want to hold you in my arms," I tell her and motion for her to come lie next to me.

She jostles from foot to foot, chewing on her bottom lip while her eyes dart around the barn as if she's going to see something that makes it all okay. "Just ten minutes," she says, finally walking back toward me and taking a seat on the blanket next to me.

I wrap an arm around her middle and pull her down against my side as I relax. "I love you."

"I love you too," she says back to me, staring up at me from the crook of my arm.

There's a sadness that hangs in the air because we both know we're going to be separated for a while. We'll still see each other in school; there's nothing he can do about that. However, the time we spend together after school is going to come to an end until her father decides to let her out of the house again.

"I'm sorry I fell asleep."

She sighs and traces the lines of my stomach with her

fingertip. "Don't apologize. I could sleep forever in your arms. It's just as much my fault as it is yours." She smiles softly.

There are times when I wish we were adults, on our own and not under the rules of her father. Evie and I could be so happy and content, but the bastard will do anything to keep us apart. Even if I drop Evie off one minute late, he grounds her. He's such an asshole.

My hand glides up and down her arm as I kiss the top of her head and bury my face in her hair. I close my eyes and memorize the feel of her skin against mine and the smell of her around me. I need the memories to hold on to. They will have to get me through the next sentence her father plans to dish out.

My phone on the nightstand has been vibrating on and off for the last minute, trying to pull me from the memory of my last full night with Evie before she dropped the bomb on me that she was moving overseas.

The sound doesn't wake her, and I think about ignoring it, but the way it stops and starts again lets me know it's probably important.

I slide my hand carefully to grab it without moving or causing Evie to stir. The screen almost blinds me in the darkness of her room, and I squint to make out the words of the text messages.

Mom: Your sister's in trouble.

Mom: Are you there?

Mom: Jack, call me.

Mom: It's URGENT.

I sit up, grabbing my pants and T-shirt from the floor

as I climb to my feet, and tiptoe into the hallway, closing the door behind me.

Fuck, I don't want to leave this house right now.

I grab a pad of paper that's sitting out on the counter and scribble her a message. I hate knowing that she's going to wake up alone, and I can't stomach not at least giving her an explanation.

Leave it to Myra to screw up my night. I swear, she has an Evie radar that goes off just out of pure hatred and jealousy. After I'm dressed and halfway out the door, I finally call my mom back.

"What the hell took you so long?" she barks on the other end of the line.

"I'm with Evie, Ma. What's wrong?"

"Your sister has been arrested. You need to go over there and see if you can get her out. I'd go, but…"

"I got it."

Fucking Myra.

"Call me when you know what happened. The officer wouldn't say anything to me and asked me to come down to the station."

"I will. Give me a little bit to get there."

"I'm worried, Jack." Her voice comes out strained, and I can tell she's been crying. My sister needs her ass beat.

"I'll handle it," I tell her before the line goes dead.

I stalk into the police station ten minutes later, completely pissed off at my sister. Not only did she interrupt my night with Evie, but she has my mom in a complete panic. That's what upsets me the most, what she is doing to our mother, making her worry.

I did some stupid shit in my day, but never anything bad enough that I ended up in police custody.

"Can I help you?" the officer behind the desk asks me without even looking up.

I grip my cell phone tightly, almost crushing it. "I'm here about my sister."

"Her name?"

"Myra Nelson."

"One moment." He picks up the phone next to him, still staring downward. "Someone is here about Nelson." He finally glances up at me, his eyes coming to my legs before climbing slowly up my body. "Your name?"

"Jack Nelson, her brother."

"It's Mr. Jack Nelson."

"Someone will be right out," he says as he slides the telephone back onto the base. "Please have a seat."

Not much has changed since I came here years ago to claim my father's personal effects after his death. The place makes me uneasy; the crushing memory of that time in my life still weighs on me.

I regret not being around when he died. Moving away for school had always been a dream, but I never realized how short life could be or how quickly it can end. When I was younger, I guess I thought of my parents as being invincible. They were always simply there. I never dreamed of something happening and taking either of them away from me.

"Jack," Jess says as he walks into the waiting area, looking every bit the part of a small-town, asshole deputy.

I smile politely and shake his hand, because the last thing I want to do is piss off a cop, even if it's Jess. "Hey, Jess. I heard my sister is here."

The slow, simmering anger that I've had since my mother called is about to boil over if he decides to give me any shit.

"Yep." He rocks back and forth on his feet and drags his hand through his mullet before blowing out a long breath. "Sorry to say she is."

I ball my hand into a tight fist at my side to stop myself from having a meltdown. "What happened?"

At this point, I'm annoyed with Jess way more than I'm pissed at Myra.

"Why don't you follow me where we can talk in private?"

"Sure," I tell him. Small-town police departments make big deals out of the stupidest shit, and Jess is playing it up like the best of them. "Let's walk and talk."

He opens the door for me. "Second door on the left," he says, following behind me. I expect to see Myra when I walk in, but it's just a table and two chairs. I sit down, crossing my arms in front of my chest and wait as Jess closes the door and takes a seat across from me. "Where's my sister?"

"You can see her in a few minutes. They're finishing up with her now."

I turn my head like I might have misheard him. "Finishing up with her?"

"My partner is questioning her."

"Why? She's just a kid."

At this point, I'm about to explode like a firecracker. Jess is the fuse, and this entire situation is the gunpowder. Three… Two…

"She was found intoxicated at a party. We brought in all the kids about two hours ago."

"Big deal." I roll my eyes and can't believe they called me down here for this shit. They made my mother a nervous wreck over some alcohol. *Dumbfucks*. "We got drunk all the time when we were in high school. If I remember right, you had a huge party at your place when your parents were away."

He did it more than once too.

"We received a tip that there were narcotics at the party, and we decided to raid the location in hopes of catching the distributor. This is a small town, Jack, but things aren't like they were when we were kids."

If he says Myra is behind a massive drug ring in town, I'm going to squeeze the life out of him. "Did you find anything?"

"Not as much as we hoped, but we did find drugs at the scene."

I resist the urge to roll my eyes again. "Then why was Myra arrested? Sounds like you have more shit to worry about than a kid drinking a little too much beer."

He taps his finger on the table, staring me down, and doesn't speak at first. I want to lunge at him and rip him limb from limb.

"She was brought in as an accomplice."

"An accomplice to what? Beer?" I snort and slap my knee instead of smacking his face.

"We found her in the bedroom with a boy who had three grams of cocaine on him."

I grab the edge of the table and hold myself in my seat. Even though it would feel amazing to pop Jess in the face, it would do nothing to get my sister out of here. "You still haven't said what *she* did?"

"We found residue in her purse," he says point-blank with all seriousness.

I throw my hands up in the air, and they come down hard on the table with a loud thump. "Are you fucking kidding me with this shit right now, Jess?"

"I'm afraid not." He looks cocky, but only because he's wearing the uniform and knows I can't do anything. At least, not while I'm at the station and he's on duty.

"Half the money in this country has residue on it. It could've easily transferred."

He shakes his head. "You've watched too much television."

"Either you release my sister, or I'll bring down a fancy team of lawyers that will crush this police department and sue them for every penny for detaining my sister without cause."

"I'll release her into your custody because we're friends, but you'd better get her straightened out, Jack. We may need to question her again once she's sobered up about the boy she was with tonight."

I climb from my chair and follow him when he opens the door. "I want to see her while you get the paperwork done."

"It's against regulations until we're through with her, but I can make an exception for you." He smiles as if he's being my friend, but it's just a prime example of what a douche he really always has been. I can't stand the prick.

He takes me down a hallway to a row of cells, but there's no Myra. "She's still in interrogation," he tells me. "I can leave you there with her while I discuss her release."

I don't bother with a response. Nothing I can say will make any of this any better, but with my smart mouth, I could make the entire thing worse.

"Jack," Myra says from a bench when I enter the interrogation area.

I hold out my arms, and she runs to me, wrapping her tiny body around me. "Hey, baby girl."

"I was so scared," she whispers, squeezing me tightly as if I might disappear. Tears spring to her eyes as she refuses to let me go. The makeup running down her face gives me pause. She isn't the same little girl who would follow me around anymore. She's growing up—and fast.

I remember the day she was born. Her tiny body was placed in my arms, and my mother told me it was my job to protect her. I promised my mother I would always look after my sister and keep her safe. Even when I lived away, I checked up on her. But these last few weeks, I've become distracted and lost sight of what might've been going on with her.

"I've got you." I kiss the top of her head and hug her back. "I'm getting you out of here."

She buries her face against my chest and says, "Thank you."

"But you have a lot of explaining to do, Myra. You're not getting off so easily on this one," I warn.

She exhales into my shirt but keeps herself tangled around me like a scared little girl. "I'll tell you everything."

"Damn right, you will." With the absence of my father, I need to step in and fill his shoes. He was tough but fair and never raised a hand to us. He'd use this as a lesson, telling us what could be learned from such reckless behavior.

"Good news," Jess says, walking into the interrogation room moments later. His hands grip his belt, his belly hanging over it and hiding the buckle. "She's free to go."

"We're done?" I ask him, ready to bust out of here probably just as much as Myra's ready to go too.

"Yep. But we may need her to come back in to answer some questions about the boy," he reiterates.

"You have my word," I tell him before looking down at my sister. "Ready?"

She looks relieved as her eyes fill with more tears. "I've never been more ready in my life."

"Come on. Let's get home." I wrap my arm around her shoulder, letting her bend down to grab the purse that started the problem in the first place, and head for the door. I don't bother to thank Jess because he doesn't deserve a thank you.

His department fucked up. He fucked up. He knew I knew it too. There was no way I would let them get away with arresting her, processing her, and questioning her without a parent at her side and have it not end in some sort of lawsuit. I'm not sue-happy, but when it comes to my sister, I'd rain down hellfire to keep her safe and happy.

The ride home is quiet. She stares out the window, and I mull over my first words to her in my head. What would my father say at a time like this? I don't want to judge her or make her feel even guiltier. I did some shit in my day, but luckily, I never got caught.

"Ready to talk?" I've given her space and time to think about what she's done. The way she molded her body against the door and stared out the window told me she'd been thinking about the entire situation. Myra can be a pain in the ass, but she's never been a complete brat. She's good at her core, but like every rebellious teenager, she's pulling some shit to test her boundaries and mine.

She glances in my direction for a moment before staring out the front window. "I swear I wasn't doing drugs, Jack."

"I believe you. But what happened?" I need her to know I am on her side. Yelling at her and calling her an idiot won't get us anywhere.

"A kid that used to go to my school, Cory, asked me on a date tonight. He told me that there was a party and that it was supposed to be the event of the year. So, I said I'd go with him."

I grip the steering wheel tighter and make a mental note that I'll probably want to kick Cory's ass at some point. "Go on."

"Well," she says, pausing and mashing her hands together in her lap. "I didn't know he did drugs. He asked if he could put a few things in my purse when we got there. You know, for safekeeping because there were so many people."

"Did you even ask what he wanted to put in there,

Myra?" I want to ask her how she could be so dumb, but I keep my cool. She's young and learning.

Her head moves side to side slightly. "No. I didn't even think about asking him that."

"Don't ever let anyone put anything in your purse. You could've been arrested for possession if the cops found it inside."

"It was close." She blows out a shaky breath before continuing. "Cory and I were upstairs when the cops busted through the door. Cory snatched my purse and ran to the bathroom, trying to get rid of whatever he had inside, but the police got to him first."

"He had cocaine inside. Your purse tested positive for residue."

"Fuck," she groans and shakes her head, staring down at her lap and avoiding all eye contact with me. Tears pool and run down her face as she weeps silently.

I keep my eyes on the road and figure she's making herself miserable enough. When my mother gets ahold of her, she's going to have hell to pay anyway. "Don't ever give someone the ability to put you in that situation. You could've been in serious trouble that not even I could've gotten you out of, but you got lucky."

"Yeah," she whispers with a hiccup.

We pull in to the driveway, but she doesn't move. I know she's scared to go inside. My mom has a temper even though at times she seems calm and serene. "Ma's going to beat me for this one."

"She won't," I say, and I can't hide my smile. "Let me ask you this, Myra. You're not planning to see this Cory douche again, are you?"

She turns her head and gives me a look that answers the question immediately. "I want no part of anyone who's involved in drugs, Jack. I seriously didn't know he was into that shit."

I want to believe her, but it's a small town, and people talk. There's no way she attended the same school with a whopping enrollment of four hundred kids and she didn't know. Kids talk more than adults, and in our closed-off slice of heaven, there are no secrets. "Good, 'cause I'd hate to have to go to jail for beating an underage kid to death."

She rolls her eyes and smiles. "He's not worth it."

"He's going to be in a lot of trouble. He's at an age where they'll probably charge him as an adult. It's time for you to grow up, Myra. You're not a little girl anymore. With age comes more responsibilities, and problems get bigger too. You can't pass everything off on being a stupid kid. You know what I mean?"

"I know, Jack." She yawns. "I get it. I promise, I understand how bad this could have been."

"We'll talk more tomorrow after you get some rest."

"Only if I survive Mom," she groans.

I laugh and pull her across the seat of my truck to hug her. "You'll be okay. Promise."

"Can we…um… lie to her?"

"I'll try to break it to her gently and leave out the part about the drugs, but she may find out on her own."

"Ugh," she grumbles and rests her head on my shoulder. "I don't want her to know what an idiot I am."

I kiss her forehead, knowing that she's growing up and there's nothing I can do to stop it. "Just don't do it again."

All I can do is help guide her and set her on a path to success.

"I won't. Lesson learned."

I walk in front of her as we enter the house. My mom's sitting on the stairway in her robe with her hands clasped tightly in her lap. Myra digs her fingers into my side as she peeks around my body and catches a glimpse of our mother.

"What happened?" Mom asks, pushing herself off the stairs and coming in our direction.

Normally, I'd be scared, even for Myra, but I can see Ma's not mad, she's scared. "Just a typical teenage party. No big deal. The cops were being assholes."

"Myra, baby," Ma says when Myra doesn't speak or move out from behind me. "Come here."

She finally steps to the side and runs into my mother's arms. "I'm sorry, Ma."

My mom wraps her arms around her little girl and holds her tightly, resting her cheek on the top of Myra's head. "You're safe, and that's all that matters."

I'm exhausted, and it's past three in the morning. I can't go back to Evie's now. I'll scare the crap out of her. "Good night," I say to my sister and mother and leave them downstairs to talk before heading to my room.

I settle into bed and close my eyes, thinking only of Evie. I'm excited about what the future holds for us. There's no going back after what happened tonight. She's mine, and there are no denying that fact. She can't hide her feelings for me any longer.

I fall asleep with a giant smile on my face, knowing things are finally starting to look up.

EVIE

I roll over to an empty bed. I stare up at the ceiling, sulking and feeling completely embarrassed and humiliated.

"Morning, sunshine," Evan says as he stands in the doorway of my bedroom with a cup of coffee in his hand. "Jack left you a note."

I push myself up and rest my back against the headboard with a yawn as I motion for him to hand over the mug. My body is stiff, and I feel like I spent the night at the gym instead of in bed with the man I love. "Gimme that coffee and the note I'm sure you've read."

"I was hoping I'd find his fine ass in your bed." He pouts as he enters and sits on the edge of my bed, but he finally hands me the cup when I glare at him. "Did you tell him?"

I take a sip and read the note, blinking a few times because I'm still groggy. Relief washes over me as I read Jack's words. "I didn't tell him."

I'm filled with guilt over not telling Jack the one thing he needs to know. The one thing that could change everything between us. I don't want to ruin this before we even get started, but he deserves to know. I would want to be told.

Evan pats my legs through the blanket and smiles lopsidedly. "You'll tell him when it's time."

"I tried, Evan. God, I tried, but he didn't want to hear it."

"Sometimes it's better to leave shit in the past. You said you tried. What more can you do?"

I sigh into my mug. "He needs to know."

"Suit yourself, princess. Get up and get showered. We have to be at the cemetery this afternoon."

Fuck.

How it completely slipped my mind that today is my father's funeral is beyond me. I let myself get lost in Jack and pushed everything out of my mind. It didn't help that I'm so angry with my father that not even I want to attend his interment.

"Plus, you don't need to look like a well-used streetwalker in front of the town."

I gape at him in horror. "I do not look like that."

He pushes off the bed and stops in the doorway, looking back at me as he holds the door. "Have a look in the mirror, and then tell me you don't look like you've had a night of fantastic sex." He winks at me, and I roll my eyes, my cheeks flaming with heat, remembering the fantastic sex he speaks of. It was amazing.

When he leaves, I finally climb out of bed and catch a glimpse of myself in the mirror. *Shit.* My hair's a mess, basically a bird's nest, with pieces sticking straight up in the air. My mascara is smeared down my cheeks and has settled nicely under my eyes to give me that I-didn't-sleep-a-wink-last-night, raccoon appearance. Even my lips are swollen and pinker than usual. Evan was right. I look exactly like a worn-out hooker.

Even though no one is going to come, I still need to make myself presentable. With my luck, half the town will show up and start talking about me and my new appearance. It's nothing that can't be fixed with a warm shower and a lot of makeup.

An hour later, I'm downstairs in my nicest black dress and matching heels, with my hair in a smooth bun and a thick coating of makeup on my face.

"Do you want to read his obituary?" Evan asks as I enter the kitchen even though he already knows the answer.

I pour myself another cup of coffee into the mug that I carried down from upstairs. "Is all the information correct?" My back is to him as I speak.

I'm on edge and getting crankier as the minutes tick by. The cemetery is the last place I want to be today. There are too many memories, and ghosts will haunt me. I wish I could skip it altogether. I can't do that, though. I must be an adult and handle my business.

"Yep."

I shrug, closing my eyes as I take a sip of the coffee. "I don't need to see it."

"Can you handle this today?"

I turn slowly, staring at my best friend, and lean against the counter. *Could I handle this?* I really don't have any other option. I've been to the cemetery dozens of times, and today won't be unlike the others.

"With you by my side, I can handle anything," I tell Evan with a bittersweet smile.

He gets up off the stool and rounds the island to stand in front of me. He places his hands on my arms, slowly stroking my skin to comfort me. "I won't leave your side, babe. I'm all yours. Anything you want, you got it. I'm always here for you."

I place my coffee cup on the counter and rest my head against his chest before wrapping my arms around his middle. "Thank you, Evan. I don't know what I'd do without you."

"Jack," he says with a little laughter as I punch him in the stomach. "Did you have fun last night, at least?"

"What do you think?" I grin as I back away from him and grab the coffee from the counter.

"Looks like you had a better time than me."

"Oh, no. What happened? Hot doc not so hot?" I raise an eyebrow because I want to know the details. I need him to ramble on about anything except where we're headed. Death is the last thing I want to discuss.

"He's about as exciting as a piece of toast." Evan rolls his eyes. "The man doesn't even eat dessert. Who doesn't eat dessert? It's unnatural." He shakes his head and scoffs.

My nose scrunches. "Oh, shit. He's definitely not a keeper."

He shakes his head in disgust. "I can't be with someone who doesn't appreciate a great cupcake or even a cookie, for shit's sake. I had to listen to his speech about how sugar is bad for your body."

I laugh softly, trying not to make a mockery of his date or his obsession with baked goods. This is the reason I love Evan. Not because of his inability to pass up a cupcake, but because of his joy for life. Even the smallest things bring him happiness, and he's taught me to savor the small stuff because everything could end in an instant. Life has taught me that.

"Kurt lectured me the entire time I ate my red velvet for dessert. I wanted to reach over the table and smack him." His hands animate the motion. I try not to laugh, but Evan is so comical.

"Did you leave him at the restaurant? I didn't hear you come in last night."

"Nah, I figured after I listened to all his bullshit, I'd at least let him suck my cock for the hassle he put me through."

I gape at him, unsure if he's lying or not. "Seriously? Evan! You did not." I can't fight my laughter this time. He's terrible.

"Uh, yeah. You listen to that bullshit for a half hour and not want something out of it. At least he gave decent head."

I'm still gaping at him. I shouldn't be in shock. This is Evan, and I shouldn't expect anything less from the man. "Well, are you going to call him again?"

"Only if I need my cock sucked. Other than that, he can fuck off and find some health nut that doesn't consume sugar for sheer pleasure. I don't have time for that in my life. Fuck that, Evie. No time for that unnecessary bullshit."

As I finally regain my composure and take another sip of coffee instead of gawking at him, I say, “You’re harsh.”

“Says the woman who’s been pining over her high school sweetheart for six years.”

It’s my turn to roll my eyes. “You know why I haven’t moved on.”

“You’re still in love with him. I get it. Just have the balls to go after him and be done with it.”

“We have history.”

“It’s in the past. Jack wants your future. You deserve to be happy. Jack makes you happy.”

I sigh loudly and place my coffee cup in the sink because I’m done with this conversation, and it’s getting late. “Ready to go?”

“We’re not done with this conversation. I want all the details about last night.” Evan grabs the keys from the counter and walks toward the door.

I follow behind him and check my reflection in the mirror one more time before I head out to the porch and then climb into the rental car. “There’s not much to tell.”

“You’re not getting off that easy.”

I spend the next ten minutes going into detail after Evan harasses me for more than I want to share. He doesn’t only want to know about Jack’s size, but shape, girth, and everything.

“Damn, girl. You better hold on to that one,” he says after I lay it all out.

“I don’t know, Evan. I haven’t told him anything yet. I know he’s going to freak out. I don’t think my heart can handle losing him again.”

The very thought of never seeing Jack again makes my

chest ache. I survived for six years without him, but it wasn't easy. Now that he's back in my life, even in a small way, I can't imagine never seeing him again. Especially not after last night. We had chemistry. Our bodies knew what to do, and he was right that this time was so much better than when we were teenagers.

"He'll be okay, Evie. Trust me. When someone loves you like he does, he'll look to the future instead of the past."

I stare out the window as we pull into the cemetery. I hope Evan is right. The only two people I have left in this world that I love are him and Jack. I can't imagine losing another person and surviving.

My heart beats erratically as we pass by the row where my family plot sits. My palms begin to sweat, and I rub them together out of nervousness. Yesterday, I felt on top of the world in Jack's arms, and today, there's a dark cloud hanging above me that makes all the happiness of yesterday evaporate.

When he learns what happened, he may never look at me again. All I will be left with are the memories. I don't want that. I want him.

JACK

When I finally make my way downstairs, my mother and Myra are sitting at the table drinking coffee like last night never happened.

"Good morning."

"You're in a good mood," Myra says as I pour myself a cup of coffee.

"What's not to be happy about? The sun is shining, the birds are chirping, my two favorite ladies are getting along, and I spent time with the woman I love last night." I grin.

Myra stares at me as I sit down across from her. "You were with Evie last night?"

"Yep." I pop the P as I point at her. "Your little shenanigans interrupted us."

She frowns and seems genuinely apologetic, which isn't the norm when it comes to anything about Evie. "I'm sorry."

"It's okay. I have all day today to spend with her." I

smile brightly and lean over to kiss my mom on the head. "You doing okay, Ma?"

"I'm fine, sweetheart. Myra is safe, and you're here and happy."

I get serious for a minute. "Ma, I want to talk to you about something."

Myra stops typing on her phone and peers up at me with curiosity. She is probably afraid I am going to rat her out, but I wouldn't do that. I gave her my word as long as she never gets mixed up like that again.

Ma touches my arm. "What's wrong, Jack?"

"Nothing. I've been doing a lot of thinking lately, and I want to buy the farm from you."

Her eyes widen like large saucers, and she gasps, grasping her chest with her hand. "You want to what?"

"Buy the farm. The whole forty acres," I tell her before blowing on my coffee and taking a sip, careful not to burn my mouth.

"Why?" she asks, still looking gobsmacked.

"Philly has never felt like home."

"Plus, Evie's here," Myra adds with a small smirk.

"That too. I want to settle down and raise my kids here."

Myra's body rocks backward like my words are a direct hit. "Kids?"

"Future kids," I correct myself.

"What am I missing?" Ma asks, looking at Myra and then back to me.

"I'm so excited," Myra says, fist-pumping the air. "You're moving back."

"Evie and I are together again, and we're going to need

someplace to settle down and raise a family. We started here and have so many great memories. There's nowhere else I'd rather be, Ma."

"The farm is worth over a million dollars, Jack. It's too much."

I wave her off. She still doesn't understand that I own my business, and it's a successful one at that. "Ma, I can afford it. The business is doing amazing."

I know what I want. What my life has been missing. Being with Evie last night put everything into perspective for me.

She scrunches her nose as she stares at me. "But you barely ever work. I don't understand how you make money."

"People buy the stuff online, and we have employees that fill the orders. Right now, it works like a well-oiled machine. I got this, Ma. Don't worry."

"I just don't understand technology."

"Thank God you're not my target audience."

"What?" She gawks at me.

Myra snorts, almost spilling her coffee all over the place. "I'll explain it to you someday, Ma. One thing at a time. Don't overwhelm the woman, Jack."

"If you two are a couple, why aren't you at the funeral with her?" Ma asks.

"What funeral?" My stomach twists with dread.

"Her father's burial is today at Shady Brook Cemetery."

"When?"

She holds up the local newspaper and glances at the clock on the wall. "Right about now."

Her words almost knock me on my ass. “Shit.”

What the hell?

Evie didn’t say a word to me yesterday about her father’s funeral. I’m a little heartbroken over that little fact, but maybe she figured I wouldn’t show up because I hate the bastard. But I’d be going for her, to be by her side and hold her hand. Even though he was a heartless prick, he was still her father.

I rush out of the house, not caring that I am in a T-shirt and jeans. Hopping into my truck, I drive right to the cemetery. I need to be by her side. We have been apart for six long years, but that is over now. Starting today and every day from here on out, I will always be with her when she needs me, no matter what.

As I enter the cemetery, I expect to see a line of cars near the area where her father is about to be buried. I’m shocked when I only see Evan, Evie, and a priest.

Evie is laying flowers at a nearby grave, and Evan’s standing by her side, resting his hand on her shoulder. I watch Evan and Evie from a distance before I climb out of my truck.

If I didn’t know any better, I’d think they were in love. They care so deeply for each other that there’s love between them but not the same kind of love that I have for Evie.

I can’t believe no one else is here. When my father died, everyone from the town showed up to pay their respects.

The Bailey family didn’t live in Ridge Hollow long enough to make many friends. Although, it didn’t help that Mr. Bailey was an asshole and didn’t go out of his way to be friendly to anyone. The lack of attendees at his graveside shows what a heartless bastard he was even after all these years.

Evie's holding her face in her hands, crying as I walk toward them. I remember how heartbroken I was when I lost my father. His absence left a hole in my family that will never be mended. If I could take away her pain, I would in an instant.

Evan looks over his shoulder and catches a glimpse of me. His eyes widen, and he squeezes her shoulder. "Evie."

I guess no one expected me to show up for his funeral. My gaze follows Evan's as he looks between me and the headstone, which Evie is sitting in front of, still crying.

I blink, unsure of what I'm reading.

My heart stops as I rock backward.

My mind reels from the words inscribed on the stone.

It can't… The name…

Willow Nelson
Beloved Daughter and Angel
Born 2011 – Died 2011

It can't mean what I think it means. I read the inscription once more.

Wait.

2011?

Nelson?

I rock backward and feel light-headed. My throat starts to close as I stare at the headstone in front of me. I've never been more stunned in my entire life. Evie had *our* baby and *never* told me about her.

Willow Nelson.

I feel more sadness than I've ever felt in my entire life. I rejoice in the birth of a child and mourn her death all in one breath. Moments I missed. The sound of her cry. The smell of her skin. I wonder if she looked like Evie with blond hair and big blue eyes or if she looked more like me with my golden skin and more pronounced features.

My feet are frozen to the ground, and I can't bring myself to speak. There's so many things going through my head, and my body's swaying back and forth as if the images are hitting me one by one, knocking me backward with each blow.

I can picture Evie as I remembered her years ago, alone, holding a newborn, scared.

Did she wish I had been there?

Did she want me there?

I should have been there.

She should have told me.

"Jack," Evie says after she turns to me, but I'm not looking at her.

I barely hear her speak. It's as if she's miles away, calling my name. I just stare straight ahead at the name of my little girl. The one I'll never meet and never hold. Never tell her how much her daddy loves her. I'll never be able to go back and watch her be born.

All I have is this moment.

The moment of her birth.

The moment of her death.

Rolled into one second and I'm helpless to change it.

"Jack." Evie wraps her arms around me, nearly knocking me backward and momentarily blocking my view as Evan walks away, giving us privacy. "I'm sorry, Jack. I am so, so sorry," she whispers.

I'm numb.

The shock of it all clings to me and shrouds my world in a fuzzy blanket that not even her touch can bring me out of.

"Forgive me," she says as her hand sweeps across my cheek so softly I'd think it was the wind if I hadn't seen it with my own eyes. "Jack. Please? Say something. I know you're upset with me. I can explain. I can tell you whatever you need to know. Don't shut me out, Jack. I won't be able to bear it a second time."

I blink again and try to find my words, but the only thing I can say is, "Evie."

"I didn't want you to find out like this," she whispers to me with her head buried against my chest, her tears soaking through my T-shirt.

I know Evie, and it had to gut her.

And I wasn't there to comfort her.

My heartache is so heavy it feels like there's an eighty-pound weight pressing against my chest. But I'm sure it's nothing in comparison to what Evie felt six years ago when she lost our baby.

I say the only words I can say. "I love you. I'm sorry. I'm so sorry I wasn't there for you, Evie."

EVIE

I gaze up in complete shock. The power of his words and ability to surprise me even after all these years has me reeling.

"You still love me?" I ask, swallowing down the last word because it sounds off in this moment.

For almost six years, I've lived with the burden of knowing we had a child and that I lost her. Jack never knew about her. Never got to experience the joy of holding Willow in his arms. It's my fault, and he's saying I love you?

"I've always loved you," he says, staring down at me with tears in his eyes. "I'm sorry I wasn't there for you, Evie. I'm sorry I wasn't there for our little girl."

My fingers brush away his tears, and suddenly the heartache is no longer my own, but ours. "I'm sorry I couldn't tell you. I'm sorry you never got to know her. I'm sorry I didn't tell you sooner."

"Shh." His finger covers my lips, and he wraps his

arms around me, pulling me tighter against his chest. I melt into him, feeling that I'm no longer alone in the sorrow I've contained so deep inside me that it weighs on me every second of every single day.

He lifts me up, taking me with him as he sits in the grass in front of her headstone. The very one I picked out for her when I buried my mother. I carried her urn around Europe with me, showing her everything I could until I made it back home. There's nowhere else I could leave her except for the very place she began. Ridge Hollow made her possible, and it's where Jack and I began. I nestle against his chest and stare at her name while he cradles me. For a moment, the burden of the secret finally fades.

Jack strokes my hair, sitting in silence, and I give him the time he needs, allowing him to lead the conversation. I've had six years to come to terms with the death of our baby, but he's only had a few minutes.

"Tell me what happened," he whispers against my hair.

"I found out I was pregnant two months after I left. We must've conceived her the last time we slept together. I didn't even think about being pregnant when I missed a period. I figured it was from the stress of moving and losing you." I stop talking for a moment and choke back the tears that are threatening to fall. "I thought you moved on and forgot about me. I didn't see the need to burden you with the news that you were a father."

"How could I forget about you? I sent you hundreds of letters."

I stare up at him, completely confused. "What? No, you didn't."

His hands tighten around me. “After you sent me the letter saying goodbye…”

My entire body rocks backward. “I did no such thing.”

“Evie, you did. I’d still have it if I didn’t read it so much that it fell apart.”

“I didn’t send a letter like that, Jack. You just stopped writing.”

“Your fucking father,” he growls. “He did this.” His fingers bite into my skin.

I gasp, the pieces of the puzzle finally falling into place. It’s absolutely something my father would have done. “I’m so sorry.” I apologize, but it’s neither my fault nor Jack’s.

“It doesn’t matter anymore, Evie girl. We’re together now. He can’t hurt us anymore.”

“All the years wasted.” Tears are filling my eyes again.

“Tell me about her. Tell me about our Willow.”

I clear my throat and try to pull myself back together, but it’s impossible when thinking about Willow. “She was born on April fifth and weighed five pounds and ten ounces. She was a skinny little thing but long like her daddy.” I smile up at him, and my heart breaks a little more. “She had your dark hair and beautiful full lips, but my shade of blue eyes. She was a perfect mix of the two of us. I named her Willow because we always lay by the willow tree near the lake. I thought it was a perfect name for her.”

He holds me closer and rests his chin on the top of my head. “Tell me more about her.”

I hug him tightly, never wanting to let go of him again. “She was a perfect little baby. She rarely cried and slept through the night at only a few weeks old. I used to dress her up in the prettiest dresses and dance around the room with her and tell her all about her daddy and how much he loved her."

"You told her about me?"

"I did." I clutch his shirt in my hands and feel the tears begin to fall against him. "I used to show her pictures of you, and I swear she smiled every time."

"She loved me," he whispers.

"She did."

"What happened to our baby, Evie? What happened to my little girl?"

"When she was almost four months old, I went to check on her one morning, and she was blue. I remember standing over her crib and screaming hysterically. My mother took her from the crib and performed CPR on her for what seemed like an eternity, but she wouldn't breathe. She was gone, Jack. We couldn't bring her back. I felt so powerless, and I failed her. I failed you."

I break down, unable to speak through my tears, completely losing it. Reliving that day is something I rarely do. It's too painful to think about. Even now, six years later, I can barely do it.

Jack rests his lips against my forehead and begins rocking me. "It's okay, Evie. There's nothing you could've done, baby. It wasn't your fault."

"She died alone, Jack. I wasn't holding her. I wasn't there for her when she needed me most." I cry so hard I lose my breath and can't make a sound.

"Sweetheart," Jack says and turns me in his arms, so we're face-to-face.

He cradles my cheeks in his hands and stares me straight in the eyes. "You did nothing wrong. Do you hear me? She loved you as much as I love you. She wouldn't want you to be sad."

I hear his words, but they're hard to digest.

As her mother, I should've protected my child. I've felt shame since the day I found her in her crib, her tiny, lifeless body looking so helpless and frail.

I should've been there to save her, and I wasn't.

She died alone without anyone telling her she was loved. I've felt like a failure as a mother for so long that I often forget about all the good moments I had with her in such a short amount of time.

Jack's forgiveness is like hearing the words from Willow. It's the one thing I've wanted since the day I found her. It didn't matter what my parents said or what Evan tried to tell me. I needed to hear that I wasn't an asshole from the person who created her tiny life with me.

I needed Jack's forgiveness.

I needed his words to set me free and relieve the burden on my heart and soul—and to finally feel free to be happy again.

"You don't hate me?"

He kisses my cheek softly and nuzzles his face in the crook of my neck. "I could never hate you. Not even after I thought you left me behind and forgot about me. I've always loved you."

"I love you," I tell him back because I've never meant anything as much as I mean those words.

It's always been Jack Nelson.

It'll always *be* Jack Nelson.

There's no one else in the world who makes my heart rejoice from a single touch and my skin tingle at the softest kiss. I never bothered looking for love again after I left and he forgot about me. Who else would love me like him? When you find the one who makes you feel alive, there's no one else who can ever compare.

"What about your dad?" Jack asks.

"The service is over. No one came."

"Then can we stay here for a while?"

"We can stay all day, Jack."

Maybe things do happen for a reason even if we don't understand them or can't figure out how one event brings us forward, propelling us toward our destiny.

Willow was our link. But the death of my father, the man who tore our lives apart, was the catalyst that brought Jack back into my life and me into his. I don't regret the sorrow I've had for the last six years. I just wish I'd had Jack with me to help share the burden of losing our child.

I regret not coming back sooner. Not tracking him down and finding out how he could forget about me so easily. I should've known my father had something to do with it.

When my father found out I was pregnant, he went off the deep end. It only solidified his opinion that moving us halfway around the world was the right decision. He was so mad I got "knocked up," as he said, but when Willow was born, the anger faded.

Jack and I sit in the grass, wrapped around each other for hours. We don't talk much, just hold each other and long for the time we missed.

There are no words that can be spoken to bring her

back. No words to utter to take us back in time and give us back the years we lost. We are here. In the now. With only our future before us. But we have each other.

With him, I feel like anything is possible. Maybe I wasn't destined to be alone. Maybe losing Willow was meant to happen to bring me back to Jack. If she were still alive, I might never have come back to Ridge Hollow. I never would've hit my head after Jack chased me through the midway at the festival. I wouldn't be here in this moment, in his arms, against his body, and filled with so much love that I think I might burst.

"Don't go, Evie," Jack says to me when we start to walk toward his truck.

Evan drove back to the rental house on his own. He's so good to me, and I know he understands I need to spend some time with Jack. All Evan has ever wanted is for me to be happy, and now I feel like I have a chance at finding joy with the man I have always loved.

"I'm right here, Jack."

"No. Stay in Ridge Hollow…with me."

"You're staying?" I'm shocked, but I never thought to ask him. My plan always was to leave and never to be with Jack, but as with most things in life, I need to learn to stop planning and start living.

"I am, and I want to build a life with you."

"But…"

"No buts. Just say yes," he says with so much hope in his eyes.

"Yes," I tell him. There's nowhere else I would rather be than where we began, with the only man I've ever loved.

JACK

"Have you heard from Evie?" I've been waiting outside government class since the first bell rang so I could catch Renee before class started. Yesterday, I received a letter from Evie I never thought I'd get. I had to read it at least ten times before the words finally sank in. She doesn't want me anymore. Told me to move on.

"Yeah." Renee pops her gum and looks down the hallway and waves at someone who I assume is Jess. "She sent me a letter. Haven't you talked to her?" Her eyes come back to mine as Jess slides in next to her.

They're pawing each other, and Jess gives me a once-over before the typical macho chin lift. "'Sup?" he asks before nuzzling his face into Renee's neck.

This used to be Evie and me between classes. Classes felt like they lasted an eternity, but now it's been weeks since I've even laid eyes on her. "I got a letter too. I was just wondering what she said to you and if you thought she was all right."

"Why wouldn't she be?" Renee is looking at me like I have two heads, while Jess's face is attached to her neck. There's a hickey on her collarbone that looks so trashy.

I lean back against the lockers and try not to push them apart. They're on the verge of making me gag, but I guess this is exactly how Evie and I made people feel. "I don't know. You're her best friend. Just wanted to see if she told you anything I should know."

"She's made a lot of new friends and seems to be happy."

Renee's words are like an ice pick stabbing into my chest. "That's good," I lie to her and start to wonder if I've been replaced. The warning bell blares through the halls, and we have thirty seconds to get our asses in the seats. I'm sick of watching Renee and Jess making out, and I push off the lockers, walking around them and into the classroom.

The teacher starts talking about checks and balances, and I'm zoned out until a note lands on my textbook. I unfold it slowly, trying to be as quick as possible. I glance over at Renee who's tapping her pencil against her open notebook with her head propped on her hand.

The note says, "What did she say to you?"

I debate about being truthful and clueing her in or keeping it to myself, but I decide to give as little away as I can. "She just sounded weird. I'm worried about her." Carefully, I fold it back into the tiny square and toss it across the aisle just as Mr. Spencer turns his back.

Renee's eyes move with each word and so does her

mouth. She can't read anything without sounding out the words. How she got to twelfth grade is beyond me. She starts to write, with her tongue sticking out of the corner of her mouth. She smiles for a second before folding it back up and hurling it across the row like a quarterback.

I catch it before it careens into Nancy Wagner's head in front of me. When Mr. Spencer glances over his shoulder, I still and pretend to be paying attention like the rest of the class. His eyes roam around the room before he turns back around and continues to draw the Venn diagram of the three branches of government.

"She seemed really happy. She just kept talking about all the new people she met. She said she didn't miss Ridge Hollow at all. But don't worry, Jack, I'm sure she still loves you."

I crumple up the piece of paper and drop it on the floor under my desk. It hurts too much to hear about her new friends after the letter she sent me. I can't deal with the thought of never having Evie again, and talking to Renee is only making things worse.

"Jack, this doesn't seem like a good idea," Evie says, trying to pull me away from the Rusty Nail with every step. "We were kids. Renee should've told you that I was trying to get in contact with you, but she was a selfish asshole."

I turn to face her, and she almost walks into me. "I've thought about nothing else except punching Jess's lights out since the moment I found out they lied to me. Can you understand that?"

She peers up at me and strokes the top of my hand with her thumb. "Well, sometimes it's best to let things go."

"Let go?" I hear the harshness in my voice and take a deep breath. My anger isn't directed at her but at the two assholes I know are inside the bar right now. Evie and I have avoided them for the last month since we'd recommitted to each other. "They took away the last six years of our lives, Evie."

I've never been the type to let shit slide off my back. The last thing I'm going to do is pretend that Renee and Jess did nothing wrong. They're vile people and never liked Evie and me together. As soon as they had a chance, they did everything in their power to keep us apart.

"Technically, that was my father, but they were accomplices for sure."

I push a strand of hair behind her ear that had fallen free from her ponytail before cupping her cheek in my hand. "Then let me do this. One punch right to the face and it'll be over."

"He's a cop, you know. You're probably going to get arrested," she warns me.

"It's worth a night in jail if he's pussy enough to have me arrested."

"Well, you're kind of big, Jack." She laughs softly. "You'll probably knock him out like Ali."

"If he fights back, I may not be able to stop myself. Just fair warning." I know fighting doesn't solve everything, and it changes nothing. I have my girl now, but that asshole has had this coming. He earned it.

"What is it with men and fighting?"

"We'll call this closure."

She rolls her eyes and sighs. "If they apologize before

you throw a punch, can you let it go, then? I'd much rather have you at home tonight instead of in a cell."

I lean forward and hold my lips an inch from hers. "I promise I'll do my best." A night in bed with Evie would be a hell of a lot better than a night in jail.

She smiles and gives me a quick nod, looping her arms around my neck and standing on her tiptoes to steal a kiss before I can kiss her.

For Evie's sake, I'll try to play it cool, but knowing Renee and Jess like I do, they're not going to apologize for a damn thing. Maybe I'm wrong, but people don't change their spots that easily. Especially when their asshole attitude has been ingrained in them for most of their life.

We walk inside with Evie draped on my arm like a trophy I never thought I'd possess again. I spot them at the pool table, laughing without a care in the world. They've never done good. They've always been out for themselves and don't care who they hurt in the process. I'd feel bad for Jess with Renee's behavior toward men in the town if he wasn't a worthless asshole too. In a way, it serves him right. The whole town laughs behind his back. He's a joke with a badge.

A hand grabs my bicep. "Don't," Jason says and shakes his head in warning, looking between Evie and me. "It won't end well, Jack."

"We're just going to talk," I tell him and pull my arm from his grip. "I already promised Evie I wouldn't hit him first."

"You mean, at all," Evie corrects me.

"Hey, Evie," Jason says with the biggest smile. "It's nice to see you two back together again."

"It's like old times," she says, tightening her hold on my arm. "I wanted to come and dance, but Jack has other plans."

"We can dance, right after they apologize, Evie girl."

"You know how they are, right? They're just going to lie," Jason says, still blocking our way to Renee and Jess.

He's right. Renee and Jess have never been known for their truthfulness. Anything that might impact them negatively is usually spun into a masterful story riddled with half-truths. But I can't let it slide and pretend nothing ever happened. Someone needs to hold them accountable for their shitty behavior.

"Jason, I have to do this."

He steps aside, motioning with his hand for me to pass. "I won't stop you, but you're not alone. If shit goes bad, I'll be by your side."

I hold back my laughter by biting the inside of my cheek. That's why Jason was always my best friend. The guy had my back no matter what shit went down, even when it could end badly for him. He's half my size, but he's still ready to throw down for me. "I think I got this," I tell him, "but it's always good to have you by my side, buddy."

His smile widens. "I'm not going anywhere."

"Men never grow up," Evie mutters at my side, and we both glance at her.

"Some things have to be done, Evie. We're wired differently from girls," he tells her. "We can't talk everything out."

"Don't you work at the school as a counselor?" she

asks him, cocking her head and judging him for his willingness to beat a little ass at my side.

"I am, but I'm not at work right now, and some things need to be done out of honor."

Evie walks at my side, and Jason is just a few steps behind us as we approach Renee and Jess.

"Hey," Jess greets us while standing behind Renee, who's currently bent over the pool table.

She's holding the pool stick in her hand and practically salivating at the sight of Jason and me, barely paying any attention to her old best friend Evie.

"You guys want a drink?" Jess asks when I don't respond.

"Sure, we'd love one," Evie says and digs her fingernails into the tender skin near the inside of my elbow. "Right, Jack?"

"Sure," I mutter with a fake smile.

I'll play along if it makes Evie happy, but I'm not walking out of here without saying what I came to say.

"Jason, want a beer?" Jess asks, motioning to a waitress and backing away from Renee's behind.

"You buyin'?" Jason asks Jess, coming to stand at my side.

"Sure." He shrugs. "Why the hell not?"

"Then I want the good shit, not the dollar cans," Jason tells him. "Right, Jack?"

Everything they serve at the Rusty Nail is cheap shit, but I'll roll with whatever Jason wants. I nod. "Right."

"Evie, come sit by me so we can girl talk," Renee says, finally hanging up her pool stick and sitting down at the table just to the right.

When Evie doesn't move right away, Renee pats the seat next to her, and I give her an encouraging little shove. "Go ahead, babe. It'll be okay. We're all behaving so far."

She leans over, placing her mouth next to my ear. "This isn't going to end well."

I smile down at her and laugh softly. "Just relax. Jason and I have everything covered. Trust me."

"What if I don't want to sit by her?" she asks with the cutest pouty face.

I quirk an eyebrow and figure I'll throw out the only option that would make us both happy at the moment. "I can punch him now, and we can leave."

She pushes away from me and heads straight toward Renee. "Renee, it's always so good to see you," Evie says in a high-pitched and completely fake happy tone.

"You too, Evie. I've missed you so much." Renee embraces Evie in a big hug, but she has her eyes trained on me. She gives me a wink before she releases Evie.

"Cunt," Jason mutters behind me.

"What?" Jess asks as we start to walk toward the table he's taken up residence at just a few feet away from the girls.

"Nothing, man." Jason pulls out the chair, turning it so he can straddle the back.

"So, you plan on sticking around this time, Jack?"

I lean back in my chair, studying Jess as he fidgets and taps his fingertips against the tabletop. "I am. I'm buying my parents' farm and have big plans."

"You didn't tell me that," Jason says with nothing but shock on his face. "That's fan-fucking-tastic, man." He holds his fist up for me to bump with mine.

"Now that Evie and I are back together, there's nowhere else I'd rather live and raise my family than here in Ridge Hollow."

Jess's fingers stop in midair, and he freezes. "You guys talkin' kids already?"

"I've wanted to make babies with her since I was in high school. We have a lot of lost time to make up for."

"Yeah," he says, glancing down at the table instead of staring me straight in the eyes.

Jess isn't a stupid man. He has to know that I've put together the pieces of the puzzle and know exactly what role they had in keeping us apart all these years. If he doesn't, he's about to find out.

EVIE

I keep stealing glances at Jack as Renee brags about her relationship with Jess. She hasn't stopped talking about how long they've been together and how madly in love they are. It takes everything in me not to reach across the table and choke her out.

"Sooo," she mutters, drawing out the word. "Jack wasn't upset about the baby?"

I forgot Renee knew.

"He was sad, but he understands why I couldn't tell him."

"It's a shame, really. He should've come after you. I mean, if I would've moved away, Jess would've been knocking down my door to get to me." She smirks.

"Renee." I place my drink down on the table and try to remain calm. "Let's not rewrite history. We both know what really happened."

She looks confused by my statement as her eyebrows

draw inward. “I don’t know what you mean. You left, and Jack moved on to everyone.”

“Really?” I cross my arms in front of me and feel every muscle in my body tense. “That’s how you’re going to play this?”

Her head jerks back, and her eyes grow wide. “Play what?”

Heat crawls up my neck, and my blood starts to boil inside my veins. The calm I had been trying to maintain is slipping as Renee tries to play stupid.

I narrow my eyes, practically shooting daggers at her. “I asked you to find out what happened with Jack and why he hadn’t written me, Renee. Remember that? I thought you were my friend.” My voice pitches higher than I intended, but she is really starting to piss me off now with this act.

She rubs her finger across her bottom lip, slowly dragging it back and forth as she stares at me without speaking.

“What’s wrong, Renee? Cat got your tongue?”

“Jack had moved on already, Evie. What was I supposed to do? Force him to write you a letter? Please.” She rolls her eyes.

“He already moved on?” My fingers are digging into the tabletop so hard that the joints on my fingers are turning white.

“Yeah.” She nods with an icy stare. “He didn’t seem to want you anymore.”

“You’re a liar.” A small growl escapes the back of my throat, and I feel myself slipping. The anger I’ve had building for six years is about to be unleashed, and Renee is about to be on the receiving end of my wrath.

"You never deserved him anyway, Evie. You were always too plain for him. He deserved someone better than you. He figured that out soon enough once you were gone," she sneers.

Her words are like a blow to my chest. I always wondered if she had a crush on Jack, but when she fell head over heels in love with Jess, I figured she'd resigned herself to the fact that Jack was mine. *Wrong.*

Without a second thought and almost subconsciously, I rise to my feet, cock my arm backward, and slap Renee straight across the face with all my might. The sound of the contact echoes in my ears before my hand starts to sting. Her head snaps to the side, and her hand instantly clutches the left side of her face.

There's the sound of three chairs scraping against the hardwood floor before Jack's arms are around me, pulling me back as Renee stands up and starts coming toward me.

Jack's chest vibrates against my back as he growls like a bear. "Better leash your woman, Jess."

"She's not a dog," Jess says, lifting his hands in the air, trying not to intervene.

Jack pushes me behind him and steps in between Renee and me, becoming a human shield. "Better think twice before you come at her, Renee."

"She hit me first, you motherfucker."

"You deserved that and more," Jack tells her, leaning forward and getting in her face.

I peek around him, shaking out my hand that's aching like a flaming bastard, but I don't regret hitting her. I worried that Jack would strike first, but in the end, I went after Renee for fucking up my life just as much as my father did.

She isn't anything but a low-life bitch.

"Hey now," Jess says, stepping in front of Renee and standing toe-to-toe with Jack. "Don't talk to my woman like that."

Fuck. This isn't what I wanted.

"Your *woman* has tried to get in *my* pants more times than I can count, Jess. Just ask Jason—she's tried with him too. Hell, let's ask the rest of the bar. I'm sure we can find more."

Jason nods, backing Jack up. "Yeah, man. It's embarrassing. I feel sorry for you. Your woman goes after anything with a dick."

"Fucking liars," Renee says from behind Jess, her hands tightly gripping the sides of his uniform.

"You callin' my girl a whore?" Jess leans in, invading Jack's personal space.

His body is tense under my touch, and I know what's coming before it happens. Jack isn't going to back down until he's able to get in at least one punch. One which will probably knock Jess totally on his ass.

"She's always been a piece of trash. You may be down with your woman sucking off other guys, but that's called being a whore in my book," Jack spits at him as Jason stands next to him.

I cringe because, like it or not, someone's getting a punch to the face. Jess tries to strike first, coming at Jack, but he ducks. Jason pulls me to the side, away from Jack's body, narrowly avoiding getting clocked by Jess's missed punch.

Jack rights his body and swings from the knees, moving his fist upward and connecting with the underside of Jess's jaw. Jess's head snaps backward so hard that I wonder if Jack broke Jess's neck from the impact.

Jess staggers backward, trying to find something to hold on to, when his hand misses a chair near his side, and he tumbles to the floor. Renee rushes to his side, crying over him and cradling him as if Jack's killed him.

"You okay, baby?" she whines, inspecting his face. "You're a monster. I'll have you arrested for assault." She turns her glare on Jack. "Both of you deserve to be charged."

"Go fuck yourself, Renee," Jason says, speaking on our behalf. "You two do anything, and I'll tell everyone in town about what happened last year on the Fourth of July." He folds his arms over his chest with a cocky grin, his eyes sparkling with mischief.

"You wouldn't," she seethes.

I make a mental note to find out what dirty secret Jason has on Renee and Jess. It's always good to have that information in my back pocket for future use. Knowing Jason as well as I do, I'm sure he'll have no problem telling us either.

"Try me. You come anywhere near these two, and I'll print that shit on the front page of the town newspaper."

"I always knew you were an asshole, Jason."

"Takes one to know one, bitch." He laughs.

A crowd has formed around us, waiting to see what happens and if any more punches will be thrown. I'm sure everything's been caught on video, but thankfully, Jess threw the first punch, and Jack looked like he was acting in self-defense.

Jess starts to wake, and Renee helps him to his feet. “Come on, baby. I’m going to take you home.”

“Let me at him,” Jess says, his words slurred and his eyes unfocused as his body sways. He can’t even walk straight.

Renee hooks his arm around his back and uses her body weight to keep him upright. “They’re not worth it.”

“What?” Jess questions as she ushers him to the door.

I can barely hear them speak even though the room is quiet, and the music stopped somewhere between Jess’s missed punch and Jack’s knockout. “Fourth of July,” she hisses to him.

He glances over at her, his head angled back a little as if he didn’t hear her right, but I don’t hear his response as they walk out the door.

“What happened on the Fourth of July?” Jack asks, pulling me back to his side and tucking me under his arm.

Jason laughs, holding his stomach. “You don’t want to know.”

“Like fuck, I don’t,” Jack tells Jason. “Let’s hear it.”

Jason picks up the chairs that have been knocked over and motions for the waitress. Within seconds, the music’s playing again, and there’s a woman making goo-goo eyes at Jason and standing at our table.

The waitress leans over extra far in front of him and gives him a good look at her tits. Jason’s eyes twinkle, and the corner of his mouth tips up into a wicked grin. “Whatcha doin’ later, sweetheart?”

“Anything you want, handsome,” she flirts.

The woman is still bent over, and he runs his index finger down the seam of her breasts. “I plan to be doin’ you.”

“I get off at two,” she says before licking her top lip slowly and teasingly dragging her tongue across the bottom one.

“I plan to get off by three.” He winks at us, and I shake my head. He’s a terrible flirt.

After he smacks her on the ass, sending her away, he finally says, “That’s Tracy…”

“Yep. Saw her name tag,” Jack says.

“She’s my girlfriend, you know. She’s a hot piece of ass,” he says, raising his glass to me. Tracy is a gorgeous woman. Good for Jason. It’s nice to see he still has his charm.

“Some things never change.” Jack shakes his head with a chuckle, smiling at his friend.

“What?” He gives Jack a shocked face, but he doesn’t know exactly what he’s talking about.

“Nothing, man.”

Jason always had girls falling all over him. Usually, he never even had time to memorize her name before he moved on to the next. The man had a little black book that rivaled the biggest phone books in the county. He was the male slut at Ridge Hollow High and wore that honor like a badge he earned in Boy Scouts.

Renee had written to me and told me that Jack was quickly catching up with Jason in my absence. I remember being crushed when I read her letter. The thought of Jack being with anyone else and moving on so quickly had devastated me.

But knowing what I know now, I wonder if her words were even true. It shouldn't matter. Jack thought I had left him and turned my back on him. He was doing what the letter my father wrote to him had told him to…move on without me. That's what Jack thought I wanted him to do even though it couldn't have been further from the truth. I can't hold the past against him. We are moving forward and working on the future we deserve.

JACK

Jason convinced us to blow town for a few days to let the dust settle and for Jess and Renee to calm down. I couldn't think of anything better than to take Evie back to Philly and show her my life and business.

"I was here a few years ago," Evie says, staring out the front window of my pickup truck as the buildings go by. "It's a beautiful place to live. Are you sure you don't want to stay here?"

"I've never been so sure about anything in my life. This isn't the place to raise a family."

That statement earns me the sideways glance, but she skates over it. "But it's a great place to have a business."

"The city's been good to me. I can't deny that, but it's not where I want to make a life."

"I get it," she says and finally turns to me with a smile. "Ridge Hollow is lucky to have you."

"To have us," I remind her. "We're in this together,

yeah?" I squeeze the top of her thigh, close to the apex where her hips meet her legs, and she blushes.

"I'm all in, baby."

"I feel like we can make a real difference in Ridge Hollow."

Last night, I shared my vision with Jason and Evie. I'd split the parcel into four, ten-acre sites. Three would have homes—my mother's current home, one for Evie and me, and then one for Myra when she's ready to settle down. The last parcel will be for Dirty Deeds Designs new headquarters and a new recreation center for the kids in Ridge Hollow.

"There's nothing I want more than to leave a mark somewhere in the world and have something to leave my kids."

I can't imagine life without children. She's scared to do it again, especially with what happened with our daughter, Willow. I know more than anything that I want a tribe of blond-haired girls who are the spitting image of their mother, running around near the lake, playing and laughing without a care in the world.

"We can practice, Jack," she promises in a sultry whisper that makes me hot for her.

"I like the sound of that." I smirk because being in Evie's bed every night and some days has been the best fucking time I've had in years.

After everything was out in the open, we realized we were always meant to be together. We are taking everything one day at a time and living in the moment, just like Evie says she's done for the last six years.

"I'm not against a baby, Jack, but I don't want to plan anything."

"No plans, it is," I say, turning into the drive that leads to the underground parking garage of my building.

"This is where you live?" she asks and stares up at the tall skyscraper, hunched down in the front seat so she can see the top.

"Yeah, Dirty Deeds is in the building next door, so it works out perfectly."

"I thought you owned a tiny T-shirt shop," she squawks.

I can't stop the laughter from bubbling out of me. Everyone seems to underestimate our T-shirt company, but we're now one of the biggest T-shirt manufacturers in the Northeast. "Most of our sales come from online, but we do have more and more physical stores carrying our designs every day."

"I feel like such a failure," she says as we're waiting for the large garage door to open to the underground parking facility.

"Don't say that. You're not a failure, Evie girl."

"I never even finished college. I spent years backpacking around Europe with Evan and waitressing to make ends meet. Right now, I'm living off the inheritance my parents left me. I've achieved nothing."

"We're going to achieve a lot. I'm not in this alone anymore."

"I'm nervous."

I park the car in my reserved space and turn to face her, resting my hand on the back of her seat. "About what?"

"What if Cameron hates me or if we don't work out?"

Cameron has never hated anyone. Well, that's not entirely true. He hates the crazy-ass bitch he dated last year who ended up posting a fake wedding announcement in every Philadelphia newspaper because she was just a little unstable.

"Those are two different things, sweetheart. Cameron will love you just as much as I do. And we're going to work out. Have some faith. I believe in you and in us."

She twists her hands in her lap, looking down at them like they hold the answers, and rests her back against the door. "How are you so sure?" she asks, staring at me.

I scoot across the front seat and place my fingers under her chin, forcing her eyes to mine. "Because after all these years, you came back to me, and this time, no one and nothing will tear us apart. We were always meant to be together, Evie. It's just life took us on different paths, but we ended up at the same place at the same time for a reason."

"I love you."

I never get tired of hearing her say that, and I don't think I ever will. I lean forward, gazing into her eyes, and whisper, "I love you too, Evie." I kiss the freckles under her eye and move down her jaw to her mouth.

My lips touch hers as her hands slide over my shoulders, tangling in my hair with a delicious sting. I cradle her face in my hands and kiss her deeply, wanting more of her.

"Jack," someone says outside of the truck and knocks on the window. I know who it is and want to punch him in the face for his timing.

Evie pulls away and glances over my shoulder. "Guess we'll have to finish this later." She smiles.

I peer back at Cameron and glower. “He can wait until we’re done.” I turn back to Evie and start to move in for another kiss. “Where were we?”

“Come on. I’m excited to see what you’ve been up to,” she says, moving quickly to evade my kiss. She opens the door and climbs out, while I’m left with a raging erection.

I’d hoped Cameron would’ve given us a little bit of time to settle in, but the bastard missed me so much he just couldn’t wait another hour to interrupt. I watch through the window as he comes around the truck and wraps Evie in his arms like he’s known her forever. He smiles over her shoulder, waggling his eyebrows at me as he presses her chest against his in the biggest bear hug. The man has no shame.

“Cameron,” I say, climbing out of the truck and adjusting myself. “Hands off my woman.”

“But she’s just so…” His voice trails off, and Evie laughs as he lifts her off the ground.

I snap my fingers and point at the ground. “Put her down.”

“Oh, Jack, get a sense of humor,” Evie says when her feet touch the cement and she stands at Cameron’s side.

I walk around the truck and pull Evie to my side. “I’ve got one, but you don’t know him like I do. He’s a cad.” I goad him.

“Come on, man.” He punches me in the shoulder. “I’m not trying to steal your girl.”

I know that much about Cameron. He’d never try to take Evie from me. Plus, I know she’d never go for him. I just don’t like him copping a feel of the woman I love. “I know you wouldn’t, Cam. I’ve missed you, you dirty bastard." I reach an arm out and pull Cameron under my arm like he is my kid brother, completely fucking up his hair, which always pisses him off. "Been busy without me?"

He rubs his fingers through his hair, smoothing it out and growling a little at me while he does it. "Let's walk to the office. There's a few things I need you to look over regarding the property in Ridge Hollow."

"Oh. Like what?" I say, following him out of the garage with Evie firmly at my side and Cameron walking in front of us.

"Just some zoning bullshit, and I have a draft of the blueprints for the recreation center."

"They drew them up quick."

"Yep. Should be done in about eleven months depending on weather, city council, and construction."

"Whoa," Evie says, coming to a sudden stop and pointing at the corporate offices of Dirty Deeds Designs. "This is your company?"

"Yeah, why?" I glance at the building and then back to her. "What's wrong?"

"You made it seem like it was a tiny operation. This isn't a shitty warehouse. Wow, Jack. I'm in awe."

Cameron laughs. "We do nothing small, Evie."

I try to look at it through her eyes and understand why it surprises her. I guess I wasn't completely honest about the success of my business. I'm not much of a braggart. I told her that we were pretty big and even showed her our website, but it's hard to grasp an online business until you're standing right in front of it.

"I see that," she says and swallows hard. Her gaze wanders to mine. "I'm really impressed and proud of you."

Her compliment makes my chest swell with pride. All the money in the world couldn't make me as happy as seeing Evie's excitement over my success. "Thanks, love."

"I still feel like a loser." She laughs softly and rests her head on my shoulder as she stares at the office building again. "I've put everything off to enjoy life a little. You're going to make me want to up my game, Jack."

"Life is more important than things," I tell her.

Cameron groans as he opens the double doors. "You two are making me ill. Seriously, I don't know if I can put up with you every day if you're going to be like this."

I lift Evie into my arms, much to her surprise, and carry her over the threshold. I twirl in a circle and kiss her just to annoy Cameron. If he can't handle what he's seen so far, he's in for a rude awakening back in Ridge Hollow.

"Still making me sick," Cameron says, almost singing the sentence.

Evie giggles as I release my hold, and she slides down the front of my body. "Cameron, we're going to have to find you a girlfriend."

"Oh, no." He waves his arms wildly and backs away from us. "I'm not settling down. I like playing the field. My single life suits me just fine." He holds his fingers up in a mock cross.

Asshat.

Evie laughs harder, and I join in. He doesn't know it yet, but there isn't much of a field in Ridge Hollow. In under three months, he'll blow through the entire single female population within a ten-mile radius.

"We'll see how long that lasts," she says, bumping him in the shoulder playfully before he stalks off toward the offices.

I sling my arm over her shoulder and kiss her forehead. "Don't freak him out too much. He's kind of testy."

She smiles up at me. "He's going to be in trouble back home. He's in for some slim pickins. Does he know how small Ridge Hollow is?"

"No." I laugh softly. "Don't tell him either. Let's keep that our little secret," I whisper in her ear and inhale the strawberry shampoo she still uses like when we were kids.

"It's going to be an interesting year, baby," she whispers back, and she wraps her arm around my back. "So, this office of yours…" She looks around the bustling office area where employees are hard at work as we walk through. "Is it private?"

"Very." I waggle my eyebrows. "Want to christen my desk?"

She gawks at me. "Come on, babe, don't play me for a fool."

I jerk my head backward and stare down at her. "What are you talking about?"

"You've never done it with someone here?" She purses her lips, and we're back to the sideways glance.

Fuck. She's jealous.

It's kind of cute, but I don't want her to be jealous. She has nothing to be envious of. Evie is the only woman I have eyes for and who has ever truly mattered to me—other than my mom and my sister.

"I've never brought anyone here, Evie. I never cared

about anyone enough to share this much of my life with them."

Her cheeks turn the brightest shade of pink, and she bites down on her bottom lip, hiding her smile. "I don't know if I believe that, but I love you for it."

"Cameron!" I yell down the hallway toward his office, waiting for him to pop his head out.

"Yep," he says, peeking around the corner.

"I need an hour alone with my girl. Understand?"

A smile slowly spreads across Cameron's face as he looks at both of us. "Finally going to christen the place, huh?"

"I told you." I bop the tip of her nose with my finger.

Her mouth drops open.

"Don't bother us until I open the door. Got me?" I ask him, making sure I'm perfectly clear since he already interrupted us once.

"I won't knock, but I may listen," he says and disappears into his office before I can say anything back. He better not even think about it. Evie's moans are reserved for my ears only.

Lifting Evie back into my arms, I carry her into my office, locking the door behind me before setting her on the couch and covering her with my body. "I've waited forever for you," I whisper as I stare down at her.

She gazes up at me and wraps her arms around my neck. "I want an eternity with you, Jack. You're my forever. Always have been, and always will be."

I don't reply. There's nothing else left to say. Evie and I are right where we left off before she moved away. The love we have for each other has only grown, changing and evolving into something more. With age comes wisdom, and the separation brought us to this moment, this place, and this love.

Without our time apart, we wouldn't be who we are. Maybe we wouldn't have left Ridge Hollow and I never would've started a company. Willow may have been here, and that thought makes my heart ache. But we parted at a time that led us to lead lives that made this moment possible in all its perfection.

EVIE

There's a hum to Philadelphia that's almost deafening compared to the quietness of Ridge Hollow. The sound of the sirens echoing off the buildings as an ambulance buzzes down the street below wakes me just before sunrise. I kiss Jack before making a beeline to his kitchen to start the coffee, ultimately settling in to enjoy the sunrise on his wraparound patio while he sleeps.

Six months ago, I never could've imagined being here with him. It's funny how quickly life can change, especially when you're least expecting it. I had given up on love with anyone, especially Jack, a few years ago. I thought I was too broken inside to ever love again, but being with Jack is different.

He's like going home again. Home had never been Ridge Hollow, the place, but the guy I left behind there. Everything seems right when I'm with him, like anything is possible. The last six years without him feel like a distant memory now that he's back in my life. I can't imagine being apart from him ever again.

"The project is due in two weeks. We're going to try something different this time. Instead of letting you pick your partners for the assignment, we'll be drawing crayons from a bucket. Once everyone has their crayon, you'll find the person with the matching color, and they'll be your partner for the entire project. Remember, this is thirty percent of your grade this quarter."

I shrink down in my seat, unhappy with Ms. Edelman's idea of cooperative learning. I've only been here for a short time and still barely know anyone, especially not well enough to be forced to work with them.

I glance out of the corner of my eye, catching Jack Nelson, one of the cutest boys in eighth grade, staring in my direction. I try to stay calm, telling myself he's looking past me at the redhead that's sitting on my other side.

I tap my pen against my notebook, watching as it bounces off the page with a metallic click, and pray that I don't get stuck with an asshole. I don't want to start off my academic life in Ridge Hollow with a failing grade. My father would ground me until summer if that happened.

"Hey," Jack whispers, but I don't turn.

I continue beating my pen against the paper and keep my gaze cast downward as Ms. Edelman makes her way down the first row.

"Evie," Jack whispers, and I freeze.

I set my pen down, turning in my chair but still not looking up at him. I start to shake my leg, letting my foot take over where my hand left off as I gaze up at him. "Hey," I whisper back.

Jack smiles, and my breath catches in my throat. "Want to be my partner?"

The classroom is growing louder as more and more kids draw their crayon. There's nothing I want more than to be Jack's partner, but I can't tell him that.

"I don't think it works that way, Jack."

One side of his mouth turns upward into a devilish grin. "I can make it happen if you want to be my partner." He looks so sure of himself, but then again, he always does.

My heart's beating in double time at the very thought of spending time with Jack. "Sure." My voice cracks, and my stomach flips, embarrassment flooding me as my face starts to heat.

Jack doesn't laugh, just winks. "I'll make it happen."

I turn back around in my chair, letting my blond hair fall in front of my face in a way that he can't see my freak-out. Holy shit. Jack Nelson wants to be my partner. He's the one every girl in the school wants to call theirs. I grip the edges of my desk and whisper, "Oh my God. Oh my God."

"Ms. Bailey." Ms. Edelman shakes the bucket of crayons next to my head because I didn't move fast enough for her.

I hadn't even heard her approach because I've been too busy flipping out about Jack. "Sorry." I smile up at her and reach into the bucket, grabbing a crayon.

"What color did you get?" Jack asks when I don't set the crayon on my desk like everyone else.

I'm afraid to open my hand, clutching the thin wax stick like it's a secret I'm protecting. Slowly, I peel back my fingers, exposing a dandelion yellow crayon and set it down on the notebook in front of me.

"I'll find the other," he says.

I finally look in his direction. "Um, how?"

He smiles with his head half-cocked and lifts his chin. "I have my ways."

I'd give him my crayon if he asked. He probably wants to be my partner so I will do all the work while he goofs off, but I don't care. He's Jack freakin' Nelson, and he's cute as all get-out.

This is the best thing that has ever happened to me. I can't believe it. I am tempted to pinch myself.

He pulls a crayon from the bucket when Ms. Edelman walks by and shows me that it's blue, but says, "Don't worry. I got this."

Ms. Edelman sets the bucket down on her desk and claps her hands to get the attention of the entire class, which is now buzzing with anticipation. "All right, kids. Find your match," she says and motions for us to get out of our seats.

Jack peers around the room, making a beeline to the back corner where a boy stands holding the same dandelion yellow crayon as me. They exchange a few words, shake hands, and exchange colors.

He strides back to his chair with his shoulders pushed back and his chest puffed out a little bit more than before. "See? I told you I'd find a way," he says, sliding back into his desk, which is directly next to me.

I swallow, trying to find words, but nothing comes. For the next two weeks, Jack will be my partner, and we'll have to spend the entire fifty-minute class together.

I pull the rubric and instructions out from underneath my notebook and keep my eyes down. All I want to do is stare at him, but I don't want to embarrass myself, although he's probably used to girls ogling him.

"What parts do you want to do?" I ask, looking over the long list of tasks we need to complete by next Monday.

He scoots his desk across the floor, making the most godawful sound, and rests the edge so it's touching mine. "I thought we were going to work together on everything."

I try to hide my surprise, but I'm pretty sure my mouth's hanging open as I gawk at him. "Huh?"

"We're a team now, Evie girl."

My insides turn to mush with the nickname. No one has ever called me Evie girl, and the sound of it rolling off his tongue sends my pulse into overdrive and makes my belly turn in a way that I can't tell if I'm excited or about to be sick. Probably both if I think about it too long.

I give him a faint smile. "If that's what you want, Jack."

"I want more, but it's a start." He winks at me.

Jack wraps his strong arms around my shoulders from behind, resting his hands just above my breasts. "You're up early. You okay?"

I can't help but smile. "I'm fine, Jack. Just thinking."

His lips graze my cheek. "About what?"

I turn slightly so our lips are almost touching. "The first time you called me Evie girl."

"I remember," he says, but I find it doubtful.

"When was it, then?"

His arms vanish from my body before he slides into the

metal patio chair next to mine. "I remember every minute of us."

"So, then when did you call me that for the first time?" I press.

He sits there, thinking about it for a minute with a cocky grin just like he had the day he made me his project partner. "I'll never forget the yellow crayon."

"You were a determined sucker."

"I was horny, Evie. I think at that age I had a hard-on like every thirty seconds. It was ridiculous. I would've done anything to be close to you."

"Thank God you've outgrown that," I tell him, my eyes dipping to his crotch and his semierect cock.

"It's the morning. I can't control it, and you still give me the same feeling you did back in eighth grade."

"I don't know if I should be concerned or excited about that." I giggle softly, and my eyes dip to his dick again.

"A little of both," he says before scooping me into his arms and placing my body in his lap.

My laughter dies when I feel his erection press into my ass, and his finger traces a path down the front of my chest where my robe has fallen away. His hand slides underneath the silk nightgown I have underneath, and he cups my breast, placing my nipple between two of his fingers with a light squeeze.

My head falls back, and I'm flooded with need. Squirming against his erection, I crave for him to be inside me again even when I'm sore from yesterday.

"You want my cock, Evie girl?" he growls against the delicate skin of my neck as his lips blaze a path toward my jaw.

"I do," I say, but my voice is light and almost a whisper. He knows exactly what he is doing to me. He's driving me wild.

He turns my body in his arms so I'm straddling him and pulls down the top of his shorts, exposing his beautiful, hard cock. I glance around, seeing nothing but windows around us and absolutely no privacy. "People can see," I tell him and gnaw on my bottom lip as he pushes my nightgown and robe away from me.

"Let them watch us. I need you now, Evie. I want my cock in you."

I'm about to tell him to take me inside, but his thumb brushes against my clit, and I lose my ability to think. He pulls my body closer, pushing his cock into my already slick pussy with ease. My toes barely touch the cement below, and I try to find my footing but fail.

His strong hands grip my waist, controlling my movement up and down his shaft. The thought of someone catching us sends a tiny prickle of excitement through my body. I stare down at him, trying to concentrate on only him and shut out the world around us.

He twists his hips, rocking into me slow and deep. So deep that he steals my breath. I place my hands on his shoulders, and his muscles ripple underneath my fingertips as he moves. His gaze locks with mine, and I'm a goner. His piercing blue eyes bore into me, keeping me locked in the moment as I feel nothing but him inside of me. My clit grinds against his body as his cock strokes my insides, and my muscles begin to tighten. I strain to reach the orgasm that's just under the surface, but I can't quite get there at the speed Jack's pumping into me.

“I need more,” I say, digging my fingernails into his bare shoulders. “Faster, Jack.”

“Are you greedy, baby?” Jack smirks his usual cocky, beautiful grin and lifts my body a few inches from his before pulling me back down with so much force that I cry out in pleasure. “Better?” he asks.

I inch my body forward, touching the tips of my toes against the patio floor and lift myself off him before slamming my pussy down against his length. I contract around him as my entire body tightens with each stroke of his cock.

“Fuck me, Evie,” Jack whispers as his hand slides into the opening of my robe and plucks at my nipple, sending shock waves through my system.

The sensation is too much for me to stop the orgasm from ripping through my body. My movements become stunted and short as my breathing stops and every fiber of my being electrifies at the contact. He follows me, spiraling into so much bliss that we can barely keep our eyes open, but somehow, we do.

Our eyes stay locked, watching each other reach our peak.

The way he stares at me makes me feel beautiful and as if I’m the only person he’s ever loved. Jack has always had me. Even though I was thousands of miles away, he never left my heart. Being here with him in this moment solidifies my love and leaves a permanent imprint on my soul.

I collapse forward, trying to catch my breath as his arms wrap around my body and hold me tightly against his chest. Our hearts beat in rhythm, pounding in sync as though they're becoming one. "I love you," I whisper in his ear.

"I love you, Evie girl," he whispers back, and I know this is the man I'm meant to be with forever and ever. He's my always.

JACK

"Don't leave me here," Evie begs when I kiss her goodbye.

"You'll be fine. I'll be back in a few hours."

It's our last day in Philadelphia before we return to Ridge Hollow, and I have a few things to get done before we leave. Many of the things, I don't want Evie at my side while I do them either.

She grips my arms tightly. "Come on, you could use a massage."

Peeling her fingers away from my skin, I lean in for another kiss. "You need a little pampering. I have some boring business things to do anyway."

"Promise me you won't be long." She pouts, jutting her bottom lip out, and I want to bite it.

"I promise, love. I'll be back soon."

She nods slowly, her eyes flickering between the receptionist and me. "I'm ready," she tells her, finally letting go of my arm.

The receptionist motions for Evie to follow her, but before she does, she glances back at me with a small smile. I mouth the words I love you, and she does the same. Once she disappears, I head out to finish the few things that I must get done before we leave the city.

"May I help you?" the salesman asks as soon as I walk inside the jewelry store right next to the salon.

"I'm looking to buy an engagement ring."

He smiles, extending his hand as soon as he walks around the counter. "I'm Simon, and I'd be delighted to help you find the perfect ring for your lady today."

I shake his hand and am suddenly filled with excitement. "Great, Simon. I want to wow her and show her exactly how much I love her."

"Divine." Simon's thick British accent makes his statement sound less cheesy. "Do you have a budget in mind?"

"No budget. It just has to be perfect, and I need it today."

"Hmm," he mutters, walking along the glass display cases. "Do you have a shape you'd like?"

"I don't know." I stand next to him, looking down at an entire case filled with diamonds of every shape and size. They sparkle like stars in the sky.

"I like that one," I say, pointing to a ring that's rectangular and so big that I'm not sure how it'll look on her dainty hands.

"Ahh. That's an emerald cut and extremely popular." He reaches into the case and pulls it out, holding it up to the light. "It's part of our Polaris collection."

"Like the star?" I ask, and I know it's meant to be.

"Yes." He hands the ring to me.

I don't know what I'm supposed to look at, but I stare at it anyway. "I'll take it."

"It's quite pricey," he says, probably thinking that I can't afford it.

"Doesn't matter. I have the money, and she deserves the best. Wrap it up."

Simon moves quickly to wrap up the ring and run my credit card. I don't bother to look at anything else. It's perfection, just like Evie.

"Thank you for your business, Mr. Nelson," Simon says, handing me a bag with the ring inside.

"Thank you for your help, Simon."

I walk out of there a hundred grand lighter, but I don't care. I'm going to ask Evie to be my wife, and that's the only thing that matters to me. There is no price on my love for her.

I ditch the bag before I walk into Dirty Deeds Designs and place the ring box in the pocket of my blazer.

Cameron's waiting for me when I walk inside, but everyone else who works in the corporate offices is off on Sunday. "What did you do?" he asks, studying my face.

"I don't know what you're talking about." I try to keep a straight face but fail. I'm too damn happy to conceal my joy.

"I know that look, and it means you're up to something."

I reach into my pocket and pull out the box, showing it to him.

His eyes widen, and his body recoils as if I just showed him something hideous. "You didn't."

"I did, Cam. I'm going to ask her tonight."

"Jack, don't you think that's a little rushed?"

I laugh. "Rushed? I've loved Evie for as long as I can remember."

Cameron follows me into my office and collapses into the chair directly across from me. "I never thought you'd settle down, man."

"It's not settling," I tell him, relaxing into my chair and placing the ring on the desk in between us. "I'm finally getting what I want. I've waited my whole life for this. Evie is the woman of my dreams. I knew the first moment I saw her that I had to have her and make her mine."

He grabs the box, flicking open the top to expose the ring. He lets out a whistle. "Wow. You have it bad for this girl."

"Listen, Cameron, someday you're going to fall for someone, and when you do, it's going to knock you on your ass. Wait and see."

"Never happening," he mutters with a shake of his head, making a not gonna happen face.

"I can't wait to see your face when you realize there's no going back to random sex with strangers."

"Shut your mouth." He snaps the lid of the box closed and places it back on the desk, pulling his hand away like it burned him. "I like my life just the way it is. Let's change the subject. This one is boring me."

Anything having to do with a relationship is like having a taboo conversation with Cameron. He refuses to believe he'll ever fall in love. If Evie hadn't come back into my life, I never would've found someone else to love. No one compares to her and never could.

She's my one.

My only.

"Let's go over the plans for Ridge Hollow so I can leave tomorrow. I won't see you again until you come to town for the meeting with the zoning board."

"Please tell me there are a lot of hot women in Ridge Hollow."

I have to bite back my laughter; he is in for one hell of a surprise. "There are tons," I lie right to his face. "You're going to be a very busy man." I grin.

"Thank fuck," he whispers.

If he only knew.

We spend the next four hours going over the application for the zoning board to have most of the land parcel split into sections, including the one that needs to be changed to commercial use. Hopefully, since half of it will be used for a town recreation center and charity, they'll push it through without any bullshit.

"I'll be there to meet with the zoning board in a few weeks, and once they approve it, we can break ground and start construction immediately."

"You've done an amazing job with everything, Cameron."

"That's what partners are for, Jack. I think this is exactly what we need to take Dirty Deeds to the next level."

"I couldn't agree more."

His phone buzzes, and he glances down.

"Hot date?"

"Twins," he replies with the biggest grin as he types a message.

"You'd better be careful, or your prick's going to fall off."

He stands up and jams his phone into his back pocket. "I'll take that challenge. I gotta run. I'll see you in Ridge Hollow. Good luck with Evie."

"I'll lock up. Have fun tonight," I tell him as he heads for the door.

"I plan on it," he says before disappearing down the hallway.

I sit back, looking around my office and everything that we've achieved in a short time. We built a company from scratch with only a few thousand dollars we had saved. Neither of us expected it to take off the way it did even though we believed in our concept and had the drive and determination to pull it off.

It's late afternoon by the time I get to the spa. Evie's just walking out into the lobby, looking refreshed and glowing.

"I missed you," she says, wrapping me in a tight embrace.

"I hope you had fun, love."

"It was amazing, Jack." She smiles, pulling away from me to wave at the receptionist, who's watching us. "She said you were very handsome." She snakes her arm into mine as we walk out, resting her head on my shoulder.

I feel like a million bucks with her on my arm as we walk down the street to my truck. I've loved Philadelphia since the moment I moved here, but I love Evie more, and staying in Ridge Hollow with her feels right.

"Are you ready to go back?"

"We can stay longer if you want," she says, to my surprise.

I don't want to be anywhere else but Ridge Hollow. It's where we belong and where our kids will be raised. "I'm ready to go home."

She climbs into the truck, holding my hand the entire time. "Anywhere we are feels like home, Jack, as long as you're with me."

I lean in, giving her a passionate kiss. When I pull away, I brush a few strands of her hair that have fallen free back behind her ear. "I love you, Evie."

"I love you too, baby."

I can't wait to make this woman my wife and give her a happy life. Evie deserves the world.

"Let me drive," Evie begs.

"Right now?" I ask, glancing around at nothing but darkness.

"Yes. Just pull over."

Against my better judgment, I veer off to the side of the highway and get out, switching places with Evie.

"I haven't driven this truck in years," she says, gripping the steering wheel tightly.

I've had the truck since high school. We've made out in this truck more times than I can count. When I could afford to buy a new car, I couldn't part with this one. Cameron gave me a lot of shit, but the truck held too many memories to get rid of it.

Evie eases back onto the dark highway and turns up the radio, dancing in her seat to the newest hit from the Chainsmokers. I watch her, transfixed by her beauty as the headlights of the cars on the other side of the road illuminate her face.

Her eyes widen, and she lurches the truck to the right. I yell out, reaching for the steering wheel to right the truck before it starts to roll from the sudden movement, but I'm too late. The vehicle tumbles on to its side and keeps rolling. I see Evie and the fear in her eyes as I try reaching for her, but my head hits the window, and then there's total darkness and nothing but silence.

"Evie!" I yell when I start to wake.

A man pushes against my chest. "Settle down, sir."

"Where's Evie?" I cry out, terrified, hoping she's okay. The last thing I remember is the terror on her face before I was knocked out.

"She's being taken care of. Don't move until we know the extent of your injuries."

But I don't care about myself. The only thing that matters is making sure she's okay. I have to get to her. I need to see her. I try to move again and realize I can't. My body is strapped to a board, and there's a neck brace stopping me from turning my head. "Is she okay?"

"I'm sure she's fine, sir."

"Evie!" I yell out to her, waiting to hear her response but hear nothing in return. "Where is she? Where's Evie?"

"Let's go," the paramedic says to someone, and suddenly I'm in the air, moving toward a waiting ambulance.

I try to look around and catch a glimpse of her, but with the neck brace and straps, it's impossible.

"Evie!" I yell again and keep yelling, struggling against the restraints until they slam the doors of the ambulance. My throat is hoarse, but I don't care. She has to be all right. She just has to be. "Evie, honey!"

"Someone sedate him please," a deep voice orders.

"No!" I yell, but it's no use. I feel the needle prick in my arm, dragging me back into the darkness.

EVIE

Every muscle in my body aches as my eyes flutter open. I'm surrounded by doctors, stripping away my clothing with scissors and talking to each other.

"Where's Jack?" I ask, but my throat burns, and my tongue almost sticks to the roof of my mouth.

"She's awake," the nurse says, looking down at me with worry.

"Ma'am, can you hear me?" the doctor asks.

I nod my head and bite down on my bottom lip. I'm filled with so much fear and dread because I'm worried about Jack.

"Are you pregnant?" he asks.

"Not that I know of," I respond as tears threaten to fall. "Where's Jack?" Please, let him be okay. I only just got him back. I can't lose him. I won't lose Jack too.

"We're working on him in another room, ma'am. When was your last period?"

I can't think of what happened yesterday, let alone

when I had my last menstrual cycle. "I don't know. Last month sometime," I guess, only caring about Jack. The last thing I remember is watching his head hit the window, and the panic that was etched on his face is burned into my mind.

"Let's get a pregnancy test on her before we do anything else."

"I don't think I am. I can't be," I whisper.

"Have you had unprotected sex since your last cycle?"

I'm mortified to be discussing this with anyone, especially a male doctor I don't know, but I squeeze my eyes shut and answer. "Yes."

"Nurse Jones, please test her blood before we proceed." The doctor looks down at me, and I don't see judgment on his face. "It'll only take us a few minutes to get the results, and then we can proceed."

"Where's Jack?" I ask again.

"I'll have someone check on him in a moment. I need to get a complete medical history first."

"I have no allergies, no past surgeries, and no health conditions. I just want to know about Jack. Please," I beg, my throat aching. "Oh God, please let Jack be all right. Please."

I stare into the hallway, wondering which room Jack is in and if he's okay. The overwhelming pain in my back and limbs stops me from moving.

I lie there, staring at the ceiling and thinking about nothing but Jack. God, I didn't even see the deer until the last second, and I should've just plowed into it instead of trying to avoid it. We never would've rolled, and maybe I wouldn't be lying in the emergency room in God knows where right now.

I'm filled with dread when I think that maybe Jack isn't going to be okay. I can't take the thought of burying him next to Willow and losing the two loves of my life. God wouldn't be so cruel to take him away from me so soon after finding him again. Would he?

I found it hard to believe in a higher power after I lost Willow. I couldn't imagine something so grand being so horrible as to rip a child from my life only months after her birth. I never thought I'd get over the loss, and I never truly did, but being with Jack has eased my grief. We share the loss together.

"Doctor," the nurse says, handing a sheet of paper to the doctor.

"Ma'am," the doctor says, pushing the bridge of his glasses farther up his nose. "It looks like you're with child."

I have no idea what else he says because all I can think about is the little person that's growing inside of me. I cradle my stomach, already in love. My eyes fill with tears at the thought of being a mom again and doing it with Jack this time instead of alone.

I gasp. "Oh my God, what about Jack?"

"Evie!" I hear Jack yelling for me. Oh God, the sound of his voice brings me such relief.

"Jack!" I try to sit up but can't. I need to see him, to touch him, and to know that he really is okay—that we're okay.

"Evie," he says, running past my room and then backing up. "God, Evie." He rushes to my bedside, grabbing my hand before peppering my face with kisses. "You're okay." He lets out a long breath.

I cry harder, overcome with relief that he's okay. "I was so scared," I whisper and let the tears come freely.

"I'm fine, baby. I was just worried about you." He kisses me again before pushing some hairs away from my face that have become matted with my tears.

"Is this the father?" the doctor asks.

Jack looks down at me with confusion on his face, and I smile up at him. "Surprise," I say with a big smile, happy tears staining my cheeks.

He gapes at me, completely in shock at the news. "We're pregnant?" he stutters.

"Yeah," I whisper and hold my breath, worried that he's going to be upset.

"I'm going to be a dad?" He glances around the room, waiting for confirmation. "I'm going to be a dad," he says, looking down at me.

"You are." I move his hand that's at my side on top of my stomach. "We're going to be parents, Jack."

"Is she okay? Is the baby okay?" Jack asks the doctor.

"I think she just has a broken ankle, but other than that, she seems to be fine besides some whiplash and muscle trauma. We can do an ultrasound to check on the fetus."

Some muscle trauma? I feel like I've gone ten rounds with a heavyweight boxer. There isn't an inch of my body that doesn't hurt, but I'm alive and Jack is okay and by my side.

Jack looks relieved at the news. "Please check the baby. We've lost one already and can't have it happen again." I can sense his fear and I am scared too, but we have each other so we can get through anything.

"Was it in utero?"

"No." I shake my head and give Jack's hand a light squeeze. "She died of SIDS." I try not to think of the loss of Willow, but it's always in the back of my mind. I will never forget her.

"I'll order an ultrasound right away and get your ankle in a cast. I'd like to keep you overnight for observation, but if you're okay in the morning, there's no reason you can't go home."

"Thank you, Doctor," Jack says without looking away from me.

Everyone leaves the room, and Jack and I are finally alone. "Are you happy?" I ask him, but I know he is. Since the moment he heard the news, he's been beaming.

"I am, but I'm happier that you're okay. I don't think I've ever been so scared, Evie. When I couldn't see you and you wouldn't answer me when I called out to you… I wanted nothing more than to get to you and make sure you were safe."

"I know."

"What happened?"

"There was a deer and I meant to swerve to avoid it, but I overdid it. I'm so sorry. It was just a natural reflex."

"Shh." He puts his finger against my lips, stopping me from finishing the statement. "It's done. We're both okay, and we've got a baby to think about now. We wouldn't have known otherwise."

"We would've eventually. Trust me. After a few months, it's not something I can easily hide." I grin.

"I guess not, but now we have something else to celebrate."

"What else are we celebrating?"

"You know," he says nervously. "The business and building our dream home."

"Right," I tell him just as a new doctor walks in.

"Good evening, Ms. Bailey. I'm Dr. Kravitz, I'm the OB/GYN on duty and want to do a quick ultrasound to check the health of your fetus after your accident."

Jack pulls a chair up to the other side of my gurney and takes a seat, but never lets go of my hand. Neither of us speaks, too scared that something's wrong and that our happiness is going to come to an abrupt end with us powerless to stop it.

She lifts my gown, exposing my stomach before squirting the ice-blue jelly on my skin. Jack squeezes my hand and watches everything carefully. I've been through the joy of seeing a baby for the first time and hearing the heartbeat, but it's all new to him.

I stare up at the dirty white ceiling tiles that crisscross the room at the clinic on base. My mother dragged me here after I missed two periods. I still denied that Jack and I had ever had sex. There was no way I would tell my mother that even if she threatened me.

My stomach's in knots as the doctor moves the cold plastic wand over my lower stomach. My mother sits at my side, motionless and quiet, but I can feel her eyes on me.

I hold my breath and pray for this all to be some cruel joke that the universe is playing on me. Jack's ignored me for weeks, and my life is a mess. There's no way I can bring a baby into this world. My parents and I are civil at best. I'll never forgive them for uprooting me from my home and Jack with only a year left in high school.

"There's the little bugger."

My heart almost stops at the doctor's words. I close my eyes to hide my tears… Everything is so fucked up.

Jack sits motionless as she moves the wand around my lower belly and stares at the screen. She presses a few buttons and moves the wand again. "See this?" she asks, pointing at the screen.

"I do," Jack says first. "Is that our baby?"

"It is, and he or she looks perfectly healthy."

"Are you sure?" he asks, clutching my hand so tightly that it starts to ache.

"Listen," she says, turning a knob until the only sound in the room is the rhythmic heartbeat of our baby.

"That's her?"

"Her?" I ask, glancing over at him.

"Her." He smiles, sounding so sure of himself, and I pray he's right. I loved being a mom to Willow and would love to have another little girl to dress up.

"The heartbeat is strong. The baby is healthy. We'll watch you both for the next few hours, but I can't imagine she won't go full term."

"Thank you, Doctor," Jack tells her, leaning forward and kissing my cheek. "I'm going to be a dad."

I start to cry, but they're tears of joy. Jack and I will finally be parents and get to experience everything together. It'll be new to me.

My parents barely helped me with Willow. I think they were punishing me in their own way for getting knocked up. But in the end, I wanted to do everything myself. She was mine, not theirs. I'm going to love this baby just as much.

"I love you," Jack whispers in my ear as the doctor wipes away the gel. I can't envision doing this with anyone else. I thought I would never love again, let alone be a mom again. This baby is going to have so much love. I can't wait to share my news with Evan. I know he will be so thrilled for me.

"I love you too."

Even though our trip home landed us both in the ER and his truck probably in rubble, we're coming out of it with the best news possible.

We're going to be parents.

Jack and I are truly getting our second chance at everything we had dreamed of and more.

EVIE

"Is it your release day?" Evan asks, standing in the doorway. I've missed him and am so glad he's here.

We've been home a week, and Jack hasn't let me get out of bed. He says it is what's best for the baby, and I don't argue. I'm only allowed to walk to the bathroom, and once a day, I can walk downstairs to sit on the couch for a few hours before he carries me back up. I've explained that I'm not breakable, but he doesn't want to hear it. He is so stubborn when he wants to be. Once he sets his mind to something, that's it. There is no telling him differently.

I cross my arms over my chest and pout dramatically. "I don't know. Did you ask the boss?"

"He had a few errands to run, and I told him I'd sit with you while he ran out. But he said he's taking you out tonight."

I sit straight up, filled with excitement and relief. "He's letting me leave the house?" I nearly clap at the thought.

I'm not used to lying around all the time. I like to be on the go.

Evan nods and comes to sit next to me. "How are you feeling, Evie?"

"I'm better. I was sore for a few days, but I'm going stir-crazy in this house." That's an understatement.

"I can imagine. You've never been one to sit around this much. Tomorrow, we're having a barbecue here."

"A barbecue?" I ask, thinking I heard him wrong.

"Yep. Jack's invited his mother and sister and a bunch of your friends. I guess Cameron is coming into town for it too."

"Hmm," I mumble, pulling at my bottom lip. "He never mentioned it to me." I wonder why he hasn't brought it up. He has been so bossy and overprotective, and I love him for it, but I am so ready to stop being cooped up all the time like a prisoner.

"He probably didn't want you to go into party-planning mode. Don't worry about a thing, though. We have it covered," he assures me.

Evan looks more tired than usual, and his disappearing act has me a little worried. We haven't spent much time together lately. I have been so preoccupied with Jack and then the accident. I miss Evan. I feel as though we have barely talked in weeks. He and I are usually inseparable.

"Where have you been all week, Evan? I could've used backup." Jack has been like a drill sergeant when it comes to getting his way. I can't seem to tell the man no. Especially when he smiles at me, not to mention the things he does to me when we are alone. The man can't keep his hands off me, not that I am complaining. Jack is a sexy beast in the bedroom.

"I've been busy with the good doctor," he mumbles, dropping his voice down low.

I narrow my eyes. "I thought you didn't like him. Hmm?" I hedge.

"He's not so bad, after all. Plus, there's that whole amazing cock-sucker thing he's rockin'." He winks with a twinkle in his eye.

I shake my head and laugh softly. "I'll never understand you."

"Since you're settling down in Ridge Hollow, I figured it was time that I put down some roots too."

I gasp and clutch his hand tightly. "You aren't leaving me, are you?"

Evan's my rock. The solid foundation in my life for years. Although I have Jack, I can't imagine life without Evan.

"No, Evie. I bought the cupcake shop, and coincidentally, it has a studio apartment on top that's just perfect for me."

I turn my head like I didn't hear him right. "You did what?" I can't believe my ears.

"It made sense," he says as if I didn't ask him to repeat himself. "I don't just want to play with money anymore. I want to own something. What the hell is better than a shop that only sells desserts? You know how I feel about them."

This is quintessentially Evan. Only he would buy a cupcake shop to feed his sugar addiction and think it's a great idea. "But you're not a baker," I point out.

"I'm keeping the staff, so I don't need to know how to

bake. I'll keep the books, and of course, be the official taste-tester." He licks his lips as if he is licking the frosting off a cupcake.

I poke him in the stomach. "Better watch out, or that amazing physique is going to get as soft as the cupcakes you'll be eating. Dough boy."

He laughs and sticks his stomach out, puffing it in a way that I've never seen. "It's okay. We'll match soon enough."

I slap his hand away and remember how big I got with Willow. I'm sure this time will be no different. "I'm going to be as big as this house." My feet were so swollen I couldn't even wear my shoes. I had to wear flip-flops.

"You're going to be stunning. There's nothing more beautiful than a pregnant woman, Evie. Especially one who is so in love."

There was nothing beautiful about me last time. I felt like a Weeble, especially after I couldn't see my feet anymore. I've seen other women who pull off pregnancy and look radiant, but I wasn't one of them.

"Says a man who will still be able to see his feet," I grumble, dreading the weight gain but excited at the same time. I am so happy I get to share in the joys of pregnancy with Jack by my side this time around. He is going to make one amazing father. I can't wait to see him holding our baby. He didn't get to hold Willow like I did, but this time, nothing will come between us. We're so in love. I'm so lucky to have such a wonderful man to love me.

"I wanted to ask you if you'd like to work at the shop with me. I could use someone I trust to help keep the staff in line. Pregnant women can be testy, but who better to have at my side than my best friend? And there are the delicious cupcakes to consider. Who can say no to cupcakes? Well, besides Kurt Baylor."

"I don't know," I tell him and rest my hands on my belly. How will I resist the temptation of all those yummy baked goods? Then another thought hits me. He said he was keeping the staff and that means Renee. "Jack may not be overly excited about me working with Renee, and I sure as hell don't want to be around her."

He waves an errant hand through the air. "Oh, I fired her already. I don't need someone like her interacting with the customers. Good riddance. None of the workers liked her either. They all seemed relieved when they learned she wouldn't be returning."

The knowledge that Renee has lost her job sends warmth through my body. It's not nice for me to be so excited, but I can't help it. Renee is trash. She doesn't care about anyone but herself. "I love you," I tell him.

"I love you too. I'd never keep her around after what she did to you and Jack. I only surround myself with nice people, and she isn't one. So, you want to work at the shop with me or what? Don't leave me hanging, Evie."

"I'd love to, but I have to convince Jack. He's so worried about the baby, I've been a virtual prisoner."

"I'll take care of it," Evan says, grabbing my hand and embracing it. "He loves you is all, but I'll reassure him that I'll keep his little one safe. I will always look out for you."

"What's he planning, Evan? Do you know?"

"I have no clue," he says, but he's smiling.

"Liar. I can see it all over your face. You know something. Don't hold out on me, Evan!"

He makes the motion of locking his lips and throwing away the key.

"Come on, Ev, At least give me a hint. One clue, please. The anticipation is too much."

"Patience is a virtue," he says, peeling back my covers. "Let's get you in a bath, and by the time you're done, Jack should be back. I have strict instructions to have you ready by six."

I swing my legs over the side of the bed and sit next to Evan. "He's a bossy fucker sometimes."

Evan bumps my shoulder with his and smiles at me. "But you love him anyway."

I sigh and glance up at the ceiling. "I do. I love him so much, Evan. He makes me so happy when he isn't holding me hostage." I grin.

"Let's get you dolled up for your big night. Get a move on, Evie." Evan holds out his hand to help me to my feet, and I take it, letting my best friend help me so I don't jeopardize my parole in a few short hours.

"If he's taking me out in the backyard, I'm going to be pissed. I need to get away from this house for a night."

"He told me not to wait up tonight. It's a good sign." My best friend grins, and I can't help but wonder what Jack is up to. I don't want to get my hopes up, but there is only one thing I can think of with all this secrecy.

Evan draws me a bubble bath as I sit on the bathroom countertop, watching him and kicking my good foot back and forth against the cabinets. I'm filled with so much energy from lying down for so long that I feel like I could do a mini-marathon without losing my breath.

"I'm going to make us some tea while you soak."

"Thanks, Evan."

I don't know how I've been so lucky to find Evan. When he came into my life, it was at a low point where I felt utterly alone. But he changed everything. He made life fun again and did everything in his power to make me feel whole again.

"Shave your bits, girl. You may get lucky tonight," he sasses.

I snort. "You have a way with words, you know?"

He runs his hand up my bare legs to drive his point home. "I like a great hairy leg, but yours is a bit prickly. I don't think Jack will approve."

I hit him in the arm before pushing him away. "Shut up and go make the tea."

"Just holler if you need me. You'll need a machete to get through that jungle, doll," he says before leaving me alone. I shake my head and get undressed.

I try to remain calm and relax while taking my bath with my broken ankle propped over the side of the tub, but I'm so excited at the thought of being out of the house that I can barely control myself. I race through shaving, somehow not nicking myself once, before letting the water drain away to wash my hair.

Evan sits on the counter the entire time, talking to me through the shower curtain about Kurt and his dreams for the cupcake shop. It's the most excited I've seen Evan in a long time. He's loved Ridge Hollow since the moment he stepped foot in the tiny town, and not only is he putting down roots, but so am I.

We have finally found our home. I have Jack, and I am hopeful for Evan's future as well. He told me he'd find love when I did. It's about time for both of us. We both deserve a lot of good after all we have been through.

JACK

"Keep your eyes closed." I lead Evie through the woods and down the path we walked a hundred times when we were younger, making our way toward the lake.

"I know where you're taking me. Why can't I look?"

Our hands are intertwined as I walk in front of her, carefully moving toward the clearing. I spent half the day and thousands of dollars to make this moment perfect. "Trust me, Evie."

"I do," she whispers.

Evie Bailey is just as beautiful as the first day I laid eyes on her. No girl has ever compared, from the sunshine in her hair down to the twinkle in her blue eyes. I would've never believed in love at first sight if it weren't for Evie.

When we're finally at the lake, I let go of her hands. "Keep your eyes closed until I say open them." I drop down to one knee, glancing around to make sure everything is just as I left it.

I had a tent set up near the edge of the lake, a place we often lay when we were kids to stare up at the stars and the same spot where I asked Evie to be my girl almost ten years ago. Under the canopy is a table with the most lavish dinner I could get my hands on in Ridge Hollow and Evie's favorite… Moo and Oink. Outside the tent is a queen-size bed with a metal framed headboard for us to spend the night under the stars. I had every detail planned out, and it only took me an entire week of keeping her in bed to pull it off.

I pull the ring from my pocket and hold it out in front of her. "Open your eyes, Evie girl."

She opens her eyes slowly, letting them adjust to the light as she glances down at me. Her eyes widen when she sees the ring, and she gasps, covering her mouth with her hands.

I take a deep breath and start the mini speech I've practiced a hundred times today. "Evie Bailey, I've waited what feels like a lifetime to ask you this, but will you do me the honor of being my wife?"

"Jack," she whispers as tears begin to stream down her face.

"I've never wanted to be with another woman. I've loved you ever since the first time I saw you, and I wouldn't want to spend my life with anyone else. I've belonged to you forever, Evie girl, and now I want you to belong to me. Be my wife."

She holds out her shaky hand to me, and the tears flow

faster. "Yes," she says as I slip the ring on her finger. It's a perfect fit and looks stunning on her hand. Everything about her is perfect. She's gorgeous, standing before me in a white slip of a dress and sexy sandals. Her long blond hair is braided and lying over her shoulder.

I stand and pull her into my arms. I kiss her shoulder and resist her mouth because once I start kissing her, I won't stop until I have her naked. "I love you, Evie."

"I love you, Jack. I've always belonged to you."

"Now we'll officially be each other's, and no one will be able to take that away from us again. Nothing or no one will ever come between us again."

She gazes up at me, and my heart seizes with the knowledge that after all these years, Evie and I will officially become husband and wife. I lean forward, brushing my lips against hers, and inhale her scent, the one I dreamed about for years.

She pulls away and looks around at everything that's waiting for her. "I can't believe you did all this. You planned all this on your own, for me?"

I nod and glance around the lakefront, proud of everything I accomplished in such a short amount of time. It's picture-perfect. "I'd move heaven and earth if it made you happy."

We're halfway to the tent when she turns to me. "You don't have to marry me because of the baby, Jack."

"Don't be silly. I bought the ring in Philadelphia while you were at the spa. I planned on proposing before I ever knew about our baby, Evie. You left once. I wasn't going to let it happen again. You were meant to be mine." We walk a few more steps, and I stop her. “Remember what you promised me on this very spot?”

“I promised we’d be together always. Forever and ever.”

“We got sidetracked, Evie, but it won’t happen again. A promise is a promise, and I’m promising you right here, right now, that I’ll always love you and will never leave your side again.”

She flings herself into my arms, wrapping her legs around my body and kissing me so deeply that she nearly knocks the wind out of me. I carry her, unable to see and moving through the grass from memory until we’re under the tent.

She slides down my body until her feet touch the dirt. “I don’t know what I did to deserve you, Jack, but I’ll spend my life making myself worthy. You’re the best thing to ever happen to me. I’m a lucky woman.”

I brush her hair away from her face and gaze into her eyes. “You have that wrong, love. I will spend my lifetime treating you like the princess you are and making myself worthy of being loved by you.”

A tear slides down her cheek, and I wipe it away with the back of my hand.

“Is this why you kept me locked up all week?”

I shrug with a small laugh. “Maybe.”

She punches me in the shoulder, knowing damn well that I had to keep her hidden to pull off something of this size in Ridge Hollow. “I should be mad, but I can’t be right now. I’m too excited to be angry with you.”

I pull back her chair from the table that’s covered in white linen and the best china and crystal I could find.

"Good. I hope you're hungry because I have a feast fit for a queen."

She sits and fumbles with the silverware as I push in her chair. "I'm starving. I'm eating for two, you know." She shoots me a sexy wink. Hell, everything she does is sexy in my eyes.

"I have your favorite."

She looks nervously at the plate that's covered with a silver dome and licks her lips. "Let me see," she says.

I pull off the lid, exposing her favorite burger and fries from Moo and Oink.

"Oh my God." She leans over the plate and takes a big whiff. "This is perfect." Evie doesn't even wait for me to sit down before she takes the first bite of her burger. "Mm," she moans as the juice and ketchup run down her chin, but she's not shy as she takes her second bite.

I can't help but laugh. Evie's always loved her food, and she's never been bashful about enjoying it.

"This is so good." Her words are garbled because her mouth is full.

I don't bother to eat.

I can't.

I'm too busy watching my girl enjoying herself as the ring I gave her sparkles on her finger. Only my girl could make eating a burger erotic with the moans of pleasure she keeps making. I'm almost jealous of the damn burger, but I will have her under me, calling out my name, soon enough.

The last six years without her disappear from my memory. We survived our past and only have our future left. Nothing else matters except for our baby that's growing bigger each day inside her.

I can't wait to hold our child.

I'm the luckiest man alive.

I have Evie, and she is mine.

Always.

EPILOGUE

JACK

ONE YEAR LATER

Evie tangles her fingers in my hair and tries to pull my face away from her body to stare into my eyes. "Jack, we have to get out of bed sometime today."

I close my lips around her clit and hum my disapproval at her statement. "Oh, Jack." Her back arches off the bed, but I pull her back down by wrapping my arms around her thighs and not giving her any room to get away. My tongue dips down, soaking up her arousal and making me a little drunk on lust.

She thought I was lying when I said I'd worship her body every day, but I meant every word of it. There hasn't been a single day in the last year that I haven't had her in some way. I find myself touching her at every possible moment. Sometimes I just need a reminder that I'm not dreaming. I don't know what I did to deserve this woman.

"We're going to be late," she says with a tiny moan

before twisting against my face, so close to orgasm that I can't stop. I love watching her get off.

I glance up at her, peeking over her swollen belly to see her flushed face. "Shh, baby. Give me a few more minutes to make love to you." My mouth returns to her body, sucking and licking her pussy to bring her closer to the edge.

"You're going to get in trouble." She barely gets the words out as her hands grip the sheets and ball into tight fists.

"I like trouble," I tease, running my tongue along the seam of her pussy lips in one slow lick. "Fuck, baby, you taste so good on my tongue," I growl.

When she's unable to lie still, I climb up her body and slide my cock deep inside her. She lurches upward, curling her body into me when I'm fully seated. I'm home. It's the only way I can describe when she and I are joined, making love to each other and reveling in the feel of one another.

I tuck my hand under her ass, tipping her hips upward, allowing me to go deeper and stroke the spot that makes her wild. Her fingernails dig into my shoulder, and her soft moans in my ear make my spine tingle with excitement. I love it when she makes those sounds in response to what I am doing to her.

"You're mine," I remind her, paying careful attention not to crush the baby bump that's between us. Evie's belly swollen with our child is hella sexy.

Three months ago, we found out she was expecting again. She turned white as a ghost at the news, but I couldn't be any happier. I plan to keep her barefoot and pregnant for as long as she'll allow me. I can't keep my hands off her or my cock outta her.

Her velvety heat squeezes my cock so damn tight. "I'm yours," she moans in my ear as I thrust into her again. I will never tire of hearing those words leave her mouth.

We haven't made it official. Marriage plans are in the works, but we want it to be when we're ready. Life has been so busy, we haven't had much time to plan the wedding of her dreams. But I will make it happen. I want it to be an event she'll never forget.

I take her slowly with long strokes, pushing my cock in and out of her with purpose and care. Her body was made to be joined with mine. I want to stay here all day, loving her, but I know there's so much to be done, and it's a special day for the entire town.

I give in to my growing orgasm, letting it crash over me, and drag her with me into oblivion. Our bodies shake together, shuddering through the waves of pleasure, both of us unable to breathe. I've never felt more alive than in this moment with her underneath me.

We're slick with sweat, and our bodies are stuck together as I hover over her with my arms shaking and my legs weak. "I love you." I gaze down at her, the mother of my children and the love of my life.

"I love you too," she says through her ragged breaths.

I roll to the side and pull her with me. I try to catch my breath as I stare out the windows over the lake. The same lake where we began and finally built our home. It feels right being here with her. It wouldn't have been the same without her. Everything in my life has fallen into place.

I can't imagine being anywhere else in this world than where I am now.

"The lake looks beautiful today." She snuggles into my side and sweeps her hands across my chest. "I'm so happy."

I smile down at her and brush my lips across her forehead. "I could be happy anywhere with you."

She gazes up at me with sleepy eyes. "I'm going to be dragging ass all day now, Jack. You don't play fair."

"I just can't keep my hands to myself."

"I have to get in the shower, and the baby needs to be fed," she groans, pushing herself up and looking down at me. "We have to be at the main building in an hour."

"I'll feed Adeline, love. Are you ready for today?" I ask her, placing my hand over hers as it rests on my chest. Being a father is amazing. Getting to experience the joy with my wife and daughter at my side… Well, nothing can compare to the beauty they bring to my life. There will always be a special place in our hearts for Willow, but we try not to let her death overshadow our future. I know she wouldn't want that for us.

"I am. You're doing an amazing thing."

"We're doing it, Evie. Everything I have is yours too." She is my equal on all fronts.

She kisses me deeply before climbing out of bed. I watch as she walks toward the bathroom. Her cute little ass is a little plumper with the baby weight, and her breasts are a bit fuller too. The way her body has changed just drives me crazier and makes me want her more. My wife-to-be is so damn sexy. Simply thinking about her turns me on.

When I start to follow her, she places her hand up and

shakes her head. "I'm showering alone. We don't have time for more, and I know exactly how you are."

I laugh softly. "I can't help that I want you. You're simply irresistible." I don't think I will ever stop wanting her. She drives me wild with passion. There isn't a day that goes by that I don't want to make love to her.

"Get me a cup of coffee while I shower so we're on time." I haven't told her I have been giving her decaffeinated. Too much caffeine isn't good for the pregnancy, and I am cautious when it comes to Evie and our babies.

I walk over to her, cupping her ass in my hand and kiss her cheek near the doorway to the bathroom. "I'll be back, beautiful."

"I'll be waiting," she says before walking away from me and disappearing inside the bathroom.

I stroll through our house and take it all in. We designed everything ourselves, and it turned out perfectly. It took months, but everything is finally done. It's built on the very spot I asked Evie to be my girl ten years ago. The expansive windows across the entire back of the house give us a panoramic view of the lake, and the floor-to-ceiling fireplace overlaid with river rock kept us warm during the cold winter nights.

But spring has arrived. The flowers are starting to blossom, and the forest around us is coming alive again. Today is the opening of the indoor recreational center that's been a year in the making.

I pour two cups of coffee and head back upstairs as I think about how much life has changed over the last year.

Six months ago, we opened a second Dirty Deed

Designs facility in Ridge Hollow, just a short ATV ride from our home.

We've hired new employees and helped breathe life back into this tiny country town. Business boomed when the news picked up the story about a new local business with Made in America products. Orders started to pour in from at least a hundred-mile radius and haven't stopped since.

Even Myra has jumped on board and is now trying her hand at social media marketing, hoping to attend Penn State in my footsteps next year. She said she wants to be like her big brother. I'm proud, but she's still a pain in my ass. She has made amends with Evie, and that means the world to me.

Almost the entire population of Ridge Hollow has turned out for the unveiling of the recreation center that sits on the edge of the property. Well, everyone but Jess and Renee. The last I heard from Mrs. Griffin, Jess is on leave from the force, and Renee has run off with a trucker. Jess had the audacity to be surprised she would cheat on him. We tried to warn the sorry bastard, but he wouldn't hear it.

When planning the event with Jason, we went all out. Not only did we hire a DJ, but we had the local restaurants cater the event to help feed the town on the company's dime. I wanted this to be the biggest event in Ridge Hollow history and something that people will be talking about for years to come.

"I can't believe all the people," Jason says as he stands next to me on the podium overlooking the sea of townsfolk before us.

I glance at him and smile. He's grinning from ear to ear and looks more relaxed than I've seen him in a long time.

"Pretty cool, isn't it?"

He pats my shoulder. "This town needed it, Jack."

He's not lying. The sleepy town has come alive with buzz since the day I announced the rec center and moving the company's main offices to Ridge Hollow.

Jason, Cameron, and I discussed how we would handle the recreation center, featuring a skate park, ice rink, and more. We decided it would be best if we offered the facility usage for free. It will be part of the charitable foundation that we run under Dirty Deeds Designs. The adults in this area barely have work, let alone the kids. We can't expect them to pay, especially if our goal is to give them something else to do during the day and on the weekends besides drugs.

I have high hopes that we're giving them an exciting and safe alternative to the drugs and alcohol that have started to plague the young people of my hometown.

"Smile," the local photographer for the *Hollow Press* says, and Jason and I both turn for the photo op before he snaps a few photos.

"Are you ready?" Evie asks, coming up behind me and wrapping one arm around my middle, cradling Adeline in the other. "Hey, Jason."

"Evie. You're glowing." She beams as he tips his head to her, and they both stare at me, waiting for my response.

"Wait!" Evan comes running up the staircase at the

back of the stage with his doctor boyfriend at his side. "You can't do this without me."

"We'd never start without you, Evan. You're one of the reasons we're here today."

"Free T-shirts for life," he says and pumps his fist in the air.

"Who are you kidding?" Evie laughs and rolls her eyes. "Your ass isn't wearing a T-shirt, especially one from Triple D, unless it's laundry day."

"I happen to like T-shirts," Evan scoffs. "I make all my employees wear them."

"Whatever, Evan. Let's do this." Evie steps to my side, wrapping her arm around my back with her love and support. I wouldn't be the man I have become without her love.

Jason and Cameron, along with Evan, stand at our side as we move toward the podium. Cameron's waving to a woman in the crowd, and she waves back with enthusiasm. It's not the first time I've seen her around, and even though I won't say it aloud, I think he's in love. *Poor bastard.* He has no idea what's in store for him, and I can't wait to say, *"I told you so."*

As I look out at the crowd, I take stock of all that I have and have accomplished. A year ago, I thought I had everything, but I was missing the most important thing in life. Someone who loves me just as much as I love her.

A man without love, even with all the money in the world, is a man with nothing.

EPILOGUE

EVAN

"Just put it in your mouth."

Kurt scrunches up his beautiful face in disgust. "I don't want to," he says through clenched teeth.

"But it's so silky and delicious." I inch it toward his mouth, trying to tempt him. "And sweet."

"Evan." Kurt pushes my hand away softly. "I can't do it." He shakes his head, but I don't give up.

"Come on. You have to do what I say."

Kurt's eyes narrow as he crosses his arms in front of his chest. "Why?"

"Because it's Christmas and I said so."

Kurt and I have officially been a couple for a few months now, but getting to this point hasn't been easy. I never thought I'd fall in love with anyone, especially a man who doesn't like desserts and sweets. I've been able to look past his aversion to anything sweet because the man has a mouth like a Hoover vacuum.

Kurt laughs softly, but he shakes his head again. "I'm very careful about what I put in my mouth."

I place my hand on his knee and give it a light squeeze. "Sweetie, you had no problem sticking my cock in your mouth on our first date."

He places his hand over mine and smiles. "Sweetie," he repeats, teasing me like he often does. "I wanted to put your cock in my mouth, but this…"

"Pretend it's my dick. It's just as sweet. I swear." I inch the red velvet cupcake toward his mouth, but he sets his lips in a firm line like a little kid trying to avoid eating their vegetables.

"What if I smeared it on my cock? Would you eat it then?" He doesn't seem amused, so I do the only thing I can think of. I stand quickly and set the plate on the couch. I'm halfway through unzipping my pants and am about to drop them to the floor when there's a knock.

"I'm saved," Kurt says, rising from the couch quickly and running toward the door like I've had him trapped in a prison.

"Fuck," I groan and refasten my pants.

Evie, Jack, and Adeline have the world's worst timing. They're five minutes early, in fact. But it's Christmas, and I can't be upset with them. Kurt has been planning this day since Thanksgiving. The man, even with his aversion to sweets, loves Christmas and has fallen just as in love with my friends as he has with me.

"Merry Christmas," Jack and Evie exclaim as Kurt opens the door, and thankfully, I don't have my cock hanging out.

Adeline screeches and leaps into Kurt's arms because

she's madly in love with him. She's just a little thing, not quite a year, but she has her first little crush. It doesn't hurt that he sneaks her all of the sweets he doesn't want to eat. No one else is willing to share their dessert, but Kurt lavishes them on her along with a million kisses.

Kurt hugs them, holding Adeline in one arm as she latches on to his neck like a little monkey. "Merry Christmas," he says.

I walk toward them and hold my arms out because I'm feeling a little left out. Evie is absolutely radiant like she's always been since the day I met her, but it's even more pronounced since she finally opened her heart to Jack.

I figured she and I would be alone, growing old together with a gaggle of cats and dogs to keep us company. I knew she'd never love anyone besides Jack, and I never thought she'd let her guard down enough to allow him back into her life.

"My girl, Merry Christmas." I squeeze Evie tightly, missing her something fierce.

"You're looking good, handsome," she whispers in my ear as Jack stands behind her.

I release Evie and reach for Jack. "Come here, you big hunk of man."

He laughs, used to my humor, and hugs me back. Evie's a lucky little bitch. "Merry Christmas, Evan." He slaps my back when I don't let go because I'm enjoying the feel of him.

"You can let him go now," Kurt says, looming over me.

"Bet he'd put it in his mouth if I asked," I reply as I let go of Jack.

"Um." Jack's gaze sweeps between Kurt and me. "I don't want to know."

Evie laughs and smacks Jack's shoulder as she stares at me. "Are you still trying to get him to eat your cupcakes?"

"Thank God," Jack mutters and drags his hand down the side of his face.

"Who wants presents?" Kurt asks, changing the subject.

Adeline bounces in Kurt's arms. Even at her young age, she knows the word because we've showered her with presents since the day she was born.

As we sit on the couch, I can't help but glance around and feel a sense of completeness.

A few years ago, I never imagined this would be my life. Ridge Hollow has become my home, and Kurt, Jack, and Adeline have made Evie and me complete. We are a unit…all five, soon to be six, of us.

No longer is it Evie and me against the world. We are officially a family.

The End…

CAN'T WAIT FOR THE NEXT CHELLE BLISS STEAMY READ?

Let her know by leaving stars and telling her what you liked about this book. Leaving a review helps other readers find new authors!

NEW FROM CHELLE BLISS

THE ENTIRE DUET IS NOW AVAILABLE!

I look over her shoulder as I take the aspirin from her palm, but I can't get a clear view of the reception area. "How are the Cozza people doing?"

She smiles, watching me swallow the pills before taking the glass back from me. "Annoyed."

I laugh.

Perfect.

"One guy is pacing around like a rabid animal." She giggles softly, covering her mouth to stop the sound from reaching their ears.

"Even better." I grin.

As I walk toward the reception area with Cassie on my heels, I feel a sense of calm wash over me. I know I can handle Cozza, and with the backing of the board and shareholders, there's no way they'll be successful in their takeover bid.

Four men are sitting, and the one that Cassie described as "rabid" still paces but his back is to me. "Gentlemen." I keep my face devoid of emotion.

Even though this feels personal, I know it isn't. They may have been trying to take Interstellar, but it isn't mine. Either way, I'll do anything I can to stop them.

The pacer stops, turning to face me as the other men stand.

Standing before me in a perfectly pressed black suit with dark gray pinstripes, a crisp white dress shirt, and a silky red tie is none other than the smooth-talking, panty-dropping charmer from last night.

Lou.

The Lou who was between my legs less than ten hours ago, giving me more orgasms than I've had in years.

I gape, unable to hide my shock.

What the hell? Nothing makes sense.

His face matches mine, confusion in his eyes as he takes in the sight of me. "Elizabeth?"

His head tilts, his hair flopping a bit in the most delicious way, before he takes a step forward in impeccable black leather shoes.

I snap my mouth shut. "Lou?"

What's he doing here? Oh God. This can't be happening.

"Who?" Cassie whispers at my side. "That's Mr. Forte. His name isn't Lou. It's Antonio." She points at him, but it still hasn't clicked.

The people in the waiting room are gawking at us.

I blink twice, wondering if he is a mirage. There's no denying that the man standing in front of me is the same man I had sex with more than once last night. We stare at each other, both considering the ramifications of the situation.

Oh, shit.

I lied about my name, but I never imagined he could be the enemy. *Why in the world would he lie about his name?*

My palms begin to sweat, and my heart starts to pick up speed as the reality of the situation hits me. Maybe he played me. I was just another pawn in the Cozza game. I rarely believe anything is coincidence.

I take a step forward, my eyes narrowing at him. "Did you know?"

He shakes his head and gawks at me. "No."

A gentleman coughs and steps in front of Mr. Forte. "I don't know what's going on here, Ms. Bradley, but we're here to discuss the future of Cozza and Interstellar. I'm Mr. Alesci, the president of Cozza's legal division." He holds out his hand, but I don't meet his eyes as I shake. I'm unable to take mine off Antonio.

I'm still in a trance, maybe in shock, about the entire Lou situation. I shake Mr. Alesci's hand and keep my eyes pinned to Mr. Forte. "Excuse me," I say, glancing at Mr. Alesci for a moment before bringing my eyes back to the sky-blue ones boring into me. "Mr. Forte, may I speak to you in private please?"

"I don't think—" Mr. Alesci starts to say before Mr. Forte places his hand on his shoulder and gives it a rough squeeze.

"Yes, Ms. Bradley." Mr. Alesci glares at Antonio but is quickly dismissed. "We'll be fine, Jim."

Turning my back to him, I let every facial expression I

wanted to make before break loose. *What in the fuck just happened?* How in the world could this be happening to me? What are the odds of the one person I sleep with in longer than I'd like to admit would actually be the one person I'm supposed to hate the most?

There's a real possibility that he played me. It's entirely possible that he knew exactly who I was when he sidled up next to me at the bar. Just because I didn't know who he was doesn't mean he didn't know who I was last night.

Antonio follows closely as we walk into my office. Using one hand, I close the door quietly, trying to avoid any more suspicion. "You knew who I was, didn't you?" My nostrils flare, and I know I'm the one who looks like a rabid animal now.

"I didn't." He takes a step toward me.

I hold up my hand, stopping him. If he comes any closer, I'll likely have a meltdown. "Stop."

"I swear I didn't know!"

The long night hasn't made him look any worse for wear. He looks more handsome than he did last night, while I, on the other hand, am not at my best. I cross my arms over my chest and stare him down. "How could you?"

"I didn't know. I swear. Why did you lie about your name?"

My teeth are clenched so tightly that they scrape against each other, making a horrible noise and making my headache worse. "Why did you lie about yours?"

He lets out a loud sigh and moves toward me, but I take a step back and bump into the door. He runs his fingers through his perfectly styled hair and inhales. “I don’t need someone looking me up online and thinking they hit the jackpot. I never give my real name to anyone unless I know them well.”

Unconsciously, my head tilts and my eyes narrow. “So, every woman you’ve slept with thinks you’re Lou?”

“No.” He rubs the back of his neck. “Some think I’m Fabio, Angelo, Salvatore, Giovanni—” he says with a small laugh.

The ENTIRE Takeover Duet is now available!

ALSO BY CHELLE BLISS

—MEN OF INKED—

THROTTLE ME - Book 1

HOOK ME - Book 2

RESIST ME - Book 3

UNCOVER ME - Book 4

WITHOUT ME - Book 5

HONOR ME - Book 6

WORSHIP ME - Book 7

Men of Inked Bonus Novellas

The Gallos (Bonus Book .5)

Resisting (Bonus Book 2.5)

Men of Inked Xmas (Bonus Book 6.5)

—ALFA INVESTIGATIONS—

SINFUL INTENT - Book 1

UNLAWFUL DESIRE - Book 2

WICKED IMPULSE - Book 3

Men of Inked spin-off series!

—OTHER BLISS BOOKS—

MISADVENTURES OF A CITY GIRL

ENSHRINE

REBOUND

TOP BOTTOM SWITCH

DIRTY WORK

DIRTY SECRET

—TAKEOVER DUET—

ACQUISITION - TAKEOVER DUET 1

MERGER - TAKEOVER DUET 2

—LOVE AT LAST DUET—

UNTANGLE ME - Book 1

KAYDEN THE PAST - Book 2

To learn more about Chelle's books visit *chellebliss.com*

ABOUT THE AUTHOR

Chelle Bliss is the *USA Today* bestselling author of the Men of Inked and ALFA P.I. series. She hails from the Midwest but currently lives near the beach even though she hates sand. She's a full-time writer, time-waster extraordinaire, social media addict, coffee fiend, and ex-high school history teacher. She loves spending time with her two cats, alpha boyfriend, and chatting with readers. To learn more about Chelle, please visit her website.

Text Notifications (US only)
➔ Text **ALPHAS** to **24587**

JOIN MY NEWSLETTER BY VISITING CHELLEBLISS.COM/NEWSLETTER

Want to drop me a line?

www.chellebliss.com
authorchellebliss@gmail.com

ACKNOWLEDGEMENTS

Usually I have a list of a dozen people I thank in my acknowledgements. Today, I'm at a loss. I wish I had a year to type all my thank yous because in all honesty, your name should be listed amongst the names. Without readers such as yourself, I don't know if I could keep going or would've stayed sane.

So, to you, thank you for reading and for reaching out to me. Readers aren't fans, you're my family too. You've propped me up on days I didn't want to get out of bed. You made me smile on days when all I wanted to do was cry. Thank you for being you and for showering me with love and support.

Thank you to Lisa Hollett, my fabulous editor. This wasn't an easy project, but you're used to my special brand of crazy. You never complain even though I'm sure you'd like to choke me out sometimes. You're not only my editor, but a friend. I love you to the moon and back and am thankful every day that you're in my life.

Julie Deaton, you're a rockstar. Thank you for making sure my shit it together and finding all the little errors that seem to plague me. You're always fast and sweet. I look forward to reading your comments with each book and value your kind words and support more than you'll ever know.

Brian, my love, thank you for being by my side. The last year hasn't been easy for you. You've kept me grounded, sane, and continued to love me during my near breakdowns. I don't know if I could've survived everything without you by my side. I love you always.

Glenna Maynard, thank you for stepping in and helping me organize my thoughts. I couldn't look at the book another second, but you rescued me and helped me pull the into shape. Your developmental editing skills were spot on and you gave me the confidence to finally share Mend with the world. You my friend are a gem and I can't thank you enough. I'm honored to call you a friend.

To my mom, I love you and thank you for being mine. We may fight because we're too much alike, but you're the most important person in my life. We've both been lost for a year now, but we still have each other and for that I'm forever thankful. Even though you use sixty washcloths a day and leave your heat on 78 degrees, I still love you. I love every quirky, crazy bit of you and I'm honored to be your daughter.

To all the people I forgot, I'm sorry. It wasn't intentional. I really should start making lists, but that isn't my style. Someday I'll get my shit together, but until then, know you're in my heart.

Love Always,

Chelle Bliss, xoxo

Made in United States
North Haven, CT
25 May 2022

19487839R00159